THE CARDIFF GIANT

THE CARDIFF GIANT

a novel

Larry Lockridge

IGUANA

Copyright @ 2021 Larry Lockridge
Published by Iguana Books
720 Bathurst Street, Suite 303
Toronto, ON M5S 2R4

Publisher: Meghan Behse
Editor: Paula Chiarcos
Cover design and drawings: @ 2020 Marcia Scanlon

ISBN 978-1-77180-424-0 (hardcover)
ISBN 978-1-77180-423-3 (paperback)
ISBN 978-1-77180-425-7 (ebook)

This is an original print edition of *The Cardiff Giant*.

CONTENTS

to my brother Ross,

in gratitude

— Part One —

SPOOKED

— *Chapter One* —

THE CARDIFF GIANT

I arrived in Cooperstown, New York, in mid-June 2003, two weeks after the Cardiff Giant disappeared. Newly hired as an investigative reporter for the Discovery Channel, I was to size up this and other weird goings-on in the famed village.

The assignment lifted the torpor of spirit that often befell me. On my own I'd done little in life, waiting to be prodded, hoping to stumble onto something. My stumbles had yielded an early divorce and a humdrum journalistic career set within the same Midwest venues that bored me even as a toddler. Cooperstown to me was exotic, and you'll see that the village was caught up in one of the few passions of my youth.

My new job augured well. I admit to a superstitious streak, and the producers were eager to have superstition confirmed. Enlightenment was bad for ratings. I set about squashing the bah-humbug aspect of my personality. Let the ordinariness of life give way to the extraordinary, the marvelous—the paranormal!

For those of you not up on your anthropology, the Cardiff Giant was unearthed on a farm near Cardiff, New York, in 1869. He measured ten feet five inches, and had a six-inch nose, a thirty-seven-inch neck, and an unnerving five-inch smile. His weight of 2,995 pounds was owing to petrification—this giant was pure gypsum.

Within hours the farm's owner had him on display, charging fifty cents each of the hundreds who came daily to gape. An imposing groin on full view made this something other than your routine Sunday family entertainment.

The discovery should not have surprised anybody. Doesn't the Bible tell us outright that there were giants in the earth in those days? The state geologist was on hand to inspect its underside when the giant, sold to area businessmen for $30,000, was hoisted off to Syracuse. There the exhibit pumped cash into the local economy. The *Syracuse Standard* ridiculed any and all skeptics. Barred from purchasing him, P. T. Barnum made a fake and exhibited it in Manhattan, setting off a public debate over who had the genuine giant. When an atheistic cigar maker from Binghamton and two inebriated sculptors stepped forward to claim the giant as a hoax, many continued to argue in favor of petrification, including the scientific community of Boston. Passed along by many owners up to 1948, he was dumped into a shallow pit at the Farmers' Museum in Cooperstown, where he lay unmolested until the night of June 1, 2003.

After checking into the Otesaga Hotel, I met with its owner, Thor Ohnstad, head of the local Chamber of Commerce. I assumed he was of Norwegian stock. A tall gangly gent of middle age, he began plugging the unmatched treasures of the village, but I sensed right away a weariness beneath his script.

"Jack, welcome to the Great American Village. You'll like Cooperstown. Home of the Baseball Hall of Fame, Natty Bumppo, the Ommegang Brewery, the Glimmerglass Opera, the Fenimore House Museum, the life mask of Thomas Jefferson and, uh, the Cardiff Giant. That's just for starters. Don't worry, no quiz. But we're down one attraction now. Hope you can lend a hand finding our giant."

I felt there might *be* a quiz—Ohnstad already seemed a noodge— but he was my entrée into the culture of Cooperstown and I needed to be receptive. In the Hawkeye Bar, I asked him to bring me up to date. We were joined by Barry Tarbox, sheriff and local pig farmer.

"Big mystery about the giant. Everybody's got a theory," said Ohnstad.

"Mine's no goddam theory," grunted Tarbox. "Aliens behind this." Tarbox was a stocky hairy man with a snout for a nose. "No sign of burglars. Aliens done it. Snuck the giant out and hoisted 'im up ter their saucer. Bastards left no trail. Took one of my goddam pigs too. Same night." He guzzled his kir.

"Why would aliens abduct a fossil instead of a real live man? And why a pig?" I asked.

"There's no telling with aliens," said Ohnstad, with a hint of the sarcasm I'd learn was his linguistic hallmark.

"Already clear why they done it, I told yah," said Tarbox. "Brought the giant back ter life—sightin's all over the county. Giant's been having sex with our women. Knockin' 'em up. You watch—a breed of giant aliens!"

"I must admit, there's no evidence against your theory," said Ohnstad. "And we'd all like to believe it. That's already two points in favor of aliens."

"Yeah, they're colonizing us. It's a plot. Worse than faggots and pod people."

I'd learn that Tarbox had run for sheriff on a "Take Back Otsego County" platform and was hostile to the usual suspects—outsiders, artists, environmentalists, gays, lesbians, and the lame—whereas Ohnstad favored an influx of capital and was liberal-minded. And yet the redneck and the entrepreneur were still oddly chummy.

"Other stuff's been happ'nin'," continued Tarbox, lowering his voice to a rasp. "Appointed extra deputies ter keep up. A crop circle over at Millhollow . . . spontaneous combustion on Dog Kennel Road . . . two nuns assaulted by an incubus near Hyde Hall . . . five Presbyterians on a picnic at Gilbert Lake saw the Loch Ness Monster . . . three Shriners on minicycles saw Bigfoot near the taxidermist's on Highway 23, but mebbe dat was just the giant. You oughta interview these folks, Jack. Find out fer yerself."

"Spontaneous combustion?" I asked.

"Yeah, by the time we got there old Farmer Buckbee was a heap of ashes. Coroner said he was just smokin' in bed, but we knew better. They couldn't find the cigarette."

"That is puzzling," I said, trying to ingratiate myself with Tarbox yet not come over as a total ass to Ohnstad.

"There's talk the Bermuda Triangle's moved here," said Tarbox solemnly.

Ohnstad rose abruptly as if he'd heard enough and punched Tarbox on the shoulder. "And can the Lost Atlantis be far behind? Jack, you know my old friend Barry may be jumping to conclusions, but it's been one thing after another since the disappearance . . . Hey, did you hear? You've got competition. Tabby and Harris—they're moving *The Morning Show* up here for the season. I for one never watch them, but it's good for business."

Tarbox excused himself. "Gotta meet with my posse. Work on our nets." Nets of varying sizes were being specially woven for the capture of aliens.

"Jack," said Ohnstad. "Allow me to give you a quick tour of the town before dinner. You should see what you're getting into."

At the time this remark seemed innocent enough. Only now, as I reflect on the astonishing events that would follow, do I see that his cautionary words contained a dark prophecy.

— Chapter Two —

ABOUT TOWN

"No town in America packs as much history and legend into so small a space," said Ohnstad, as we set out on foot. He was bigger on legend than on history. And for a tour guide, he was damned nosy, asking me about matters that were none of his business.

"Midwesterner," I replied to a question, "from Muncie, Indiana, heart of the heart of the country . . . No, not a prosperous family. My father was adjunct lecturer in geography at Ball State, an alcoholic. My mother was a harridan . . . No, got away, went to the IU School of Journalism, Ernie Pyle's school . . . No, never covered a war, mostly postal rage shootings and mall openings . . . No, not married, divorced twenty years . . . No kids . . . Yes, she was a Midwesterner too, from Des Moines, but a snob—you'd think she was from Greenwich—and bad-tempered . . . No, didn't beat me but was good at withholding and throwing milk cartons . . . quiet-spoken up to the wedding night when she yelled at me—I'd forgotten the pralines . . . Yes, you could say that I married my mother . . . No, not with anybody right now, I've been adrift many years . . . Hey, Thor, would you mind? What are we looking at?"

We had taken Lake Street past the Masonic Hall, then the home of Erastus Beadle, the dime novel king, to the source of the Susquehanna at the southern tip of Otsego Lake. "That's Council

Rock where Mohawk Indians held their powwows," said Ohnstad. "Legend has it a Christian missionary told them his god could move mountains. They dropped that rock on top of him just to see for themselves. You had one mashed missionary. Bones still there, they say, but I put no stock in it . . . Jack, where do you stand on legends?"

"Well, I'm willing to think anything's possible. I'm a reporter and follow up leads. Legends are leads."

"There's another pertains to that wall over there," he said as we walked along the river. "White Man's Wall. An Indian chief buried next to it, upright. Has a chip on his shoulder. Whenever he feels like it, he climbs out of his grave and knocks the wall down. His way of making a statement. I don't put any stock in that either, but have to say, that wall keeps falling down!" He clumsily thrust both hands out as if to stop the falling wall. "What's your stand on race relations?"

"I'm all for them. The usual liberal notions."

We walked along River Street, across from where the gallows had stood, and turned right on Church Street, stopping for the Cooper family plot in Christ Churchyard. "This whole area is haunted by Coopers," said Ohnstad, as we read the gray horizontal slabs. "Town was founded by William Cooper in 1786. Clever fellow married an heiress, bought up land grants on the cheap from ruined investors, sold small urban lots to poor folks and presided over the community like a patriarch. Then somebody brained him. Well, he may not have been brained . . . that's just a legend. Best evidence is that he did die."

"I'll take your word for it."

"His son James Fenimore lived here—our most unpopular citizen ever. Banned townsfolk from Three Mile Point, their picnic spot. Said riffraff shouldn't have access. Wrote a novel to justify his No Trespassing sign and sued six newspaper editors who called him names. He won the suits. Nice irony, the writer as censor. Hey, don't quote me. To the world, Cooperstown's a harmonious village, and up on Pioneer Street you'll find a harmonious blacksmith. The village's oldest building, the Smithy—William Cooper built it in 1786."

I didn't let on, but I already knew a lot about the Coopers. We walked north on Fair Street through Cooper Park, where the old Cooper house had stood. Now there was a statue of James Fenimore with walking stick and bowler. I beheld again in the distance the lake that the novelist dubbed "Glimmerglass." Here it was that Natty Bumppo, the Leatherstocking, teamed up with the Mohican chief Chingachgook and the giant Hurry Harry to help Hutter, Hetty and Hist stamp out heathens. Here it was that Bumppo slew obliging deer and saved the virtuous Elizabeth Temple from a forest fire.

These things happened in the penumbra of Cooper's frontier novels and were for me embedded in the landscape. During a three-week siege of teenage mumps when the family VCR wasn't working, I read Cooper's novels, musty leather-bound volumes passed down from my paternal great-grandfather. It was my one profound reading experience. This put me out of step with my generation, most of whom never read a book they weren't forced to.

There's a weighty difference for me between a fictional Bumppo and a real-life Bumppo. A real-life Bumppo would be long dead by now.

I looked north to Mount Wellington, known as the Sleeping Lion, and surveyed the water's edge, where swamp milkweed, silky willow, and cattails flourished. Surrounding the lake was the Great Forest that Cooper bequeathed to the American imagination and that his daughter Susan described with a more precise portrait of its flora and fauna in her *Rural Hours*. It was a forest of black willows, sugar maples, shagbark hickories, and red oaks. I had already absorbed this landscape in Muncie and, in my mind's eye, was now traipsing through skunk cabbage, marsh fern, burreeds, and thimbleberries. I was swatting at deerflies and horseflies and dodging the terrifying crane flies. I saw the common loons, great blue herons, mallards, red-breasted mergansers, and belted kingfishers. Also lurking Indians. I felt their eyes fixed eerily upon me, the white intruder destined to slay them.

Ohnstad was right to talk up his town. I'll say something more about what it was like for me to be here, drawing on what I already knew and what I'd encounter in coming weeks. Cooperstown was your consummate all-American village but a bit off-balanced. Only two blacks and three Native Americans in its population of two thousand. The town had seven black slaves in 1803, three of them owned by William Cooper, a Quaker not fastidious about following his religion to the letter. One of these he and his family had fun calling "The Governor" because of his elegant bearing—they even let him be buried in the family plot. Another gave William Cooper trouble: "A young wench for sale . . . None can exceed her if she is kept from Liquor." The blacks mostly cleared out of Cooperstown after the 1827 emancipation in the North. They are still gone.

As for Native Americans, they were pretty much done in by invading Europeans and their diseases in the late eighteenth century. The white invaders improved on history. They claimed that the villages and fortifications around Otsego Lake had been created not by these Indians but by a noble and vanished race—probably the lost tribes of Israel. The Iroquois barbarians had come along centuries later and destroyed this early high culture. So it was only fair in turn to destroy the Iroquois.

The white population now is mostly Irish, German, and English, with a dash of Italian, Dutch, and French. And with them comes the striking mix of architectural styles that makes the village so damned quaint. You've got your Greek, Egyptian, Gothic, and Colonial Revival, your Romanesque, your Victorian gingerbread, your Federal and Italianate brick. Nothing is distinctly American except the occasional redneck shack. Jane Clark, heir to the Singer Sewing fortune and wealthier than Ohnstad, buys up properties and keeps them spiffy. She's also kept chain retails out, so the village has remained a village. This too makes it off-balanced—no Wendy's!

For true American balance, you've got my hometown, Muncie, Indiana, subject of the Lynds' infamous *Middletown*, a sober sociological study that dubbed drab Muncie the quintessentially mediocre American burgh. No high culture, no fine art or distinguished architecture, no food you'd wish to eat, no creative leisure—just men's clubs, a work force all too sober during the day and drunk at night, the diversion of prosaic adultery, and an entire population living lives of quiet desperation.

So for me to be in Cooperstown—with its architecture, literature, art museum, chamber music, theatre, opera, and gorgeous romantic setting—was to be wholly out of my element. I was also living out an American archetype—the Midwesterner who goes East and is transformed by the vestiges of Old World culture. At forty-five, still feeling like damaged goods after my early marriage, I hoped to seize on a larger life. And for the first time in many years I had a hankering for romance.

Cooperstown has been a tourist and summer escape village since the mid-nineteenth century. Its principal fame is baseball, the all-American sport. The Hall of Fame induction ceremony in late July throws the entire town off-balance. The streets are clogged, the networks and cable companies descend, and a village tries to accommodate an invasion of people hoping for a story where there really isn't any.

Here too, I was out of my element, for I have always hated baseball. Any passion for the field of dreams was blunted when my bicycle was stolen and ceremonially burned on a pyre by seventh-grade thugs in a Little League dugout. Whenever these same thugs chose sides, I'd be the last picked. I was no good at sports. As a Boy Scout I failed canoeing merit badge, hard to do.

I'm also squeamish. If I were baseball commissioner, my first decree would be a ban on spitting. But I've got to acknowledge that Cooperstown has given us, in baseball, the emblem of our culture.

We turned on Main Street where a startling all-American ritual could be witnessed virtually every day during the season. A petulant boy wearing a baseball cap was swinging a bat at his dad. The dad in Bermuda shorts leapt and ducked and tried to placate.

This was much of the tourist culture of Cooperstown—feckless fathers, separated or divorced, trying to make amends and bond with sons through baseball. The sons always look cheated upon exiting the Hall of Fame, which is no Disneyland. "*Now* what?"

The legend is that one Abner Doubleday of Cooperstown invented baseball in 1839. One skeptic said that Jane Austen knew more about the sport than did Doubleday, who "couldn't tell a baseball from a kumquat." No matter. On Main Street, we passed on our left the Hall of Fame and Doubleday Field of Dreams. Here too I'd done my homework and knew that enshrined in the museum was the original baseball, a small shriveled brown sphere.

"Doesn't matter that radiocarbon dates that baseball 1939 instead of 1839," said Ohnstad. "People believe what they believe, and sometimes it's good for business. I'm all for that baseball!"

Just then, a redheaded boy straight off the cover of the *Saturday Evening Post* clobbered my backside with a Louisville Slugger. He must have taken me for a feckless father. He was aiming at my head in full fury when Ohnstad shoved me aboard the Cooperstown trolley and we rumbled back to the Otesaga. I was fully conscious and grateful to be alive.

— Chapter Three —

THE HORSES OF FIRE

That evening on the veranda of the Blue Mingo Grill we looked across Otsego Lake to Kingfisher Tower, a miniature gothic castle known as "Clark's Folly" after the nineteenth-century financier who felt the lake was deficient in antiquity.

"It's just for show. Nobody lives there except bats and muskrats," said Thor Ohnstad, sipping Campari and soda. "And a ghost or two. Some folks say they've been seeing light from lanterns there lately, through apertures in the turret. I put no stock in it. There's no direct access."

"I'm here to check out all such rumors. The Discovery Channel likes ghosts."

We were joined by Esther Federman, a psychoanalyst in her midthirties on extended leave from the city. Ohnstad informed me that she was seeking her roots in the nearby defunct Jewish resort town, Sharon Springs, and spending some time with her half-sister, a costumer and set designer at the Glimmerglass Opera.

"Good to meet you, Jack," she said, reaching for her cell phone. "Excuse me a minute, I must take this call . . . No, Val, that won't resolve any issues . . . It's not a healthy way to express feelings about your mother . . . No, not mine, it's your *mother's* desertion, Valerie . . . But I'm up here for the *sake* of my patients! This is a working vacation . . . No, don't listen, they don't really want you to jump, just climb back in, watch out for debris on the ledge . . . That's it, careful . . . Good going! . . . No, no extra charge for this, Val. Now take a Klonopin and call me late tomorrow morning. Shalom!" She groaned as someone put upon. "Sorry, Jack, what were you saying?"

"How do you do?" I replied.

"Poorly," she sighed. "You see I take my practice with me. I'm sure Val wasn't really out on a ledge. Every week she thinks up a new way of getting my attention. Lacan had the right idea about treating narcissists—you terminate a session after only five minutes."

"Your treatment goes a step further," I said. "You leave town and it isn't even August. But what do I know? I'm unanalyzed."

"As you know, Esther, Jack is here to cover the disappearance of our giant." Ohnstad grinned and looked under the table to make sure it wasn't there.

"What's *your* theory?" I asked.

"Thor scoffs, but I've got one. Do you know anything about the Kabbalah?"

"Sounds like a conspiracy," I replied, again feigning ignorance.

"No, the teachings of Jewish mysticism. I've been a student for five years. Fits right into psychoanalysis—there are whole books on Freud and the Kabbalah. I'm writing a book, *The Kabbalah of Everyday Life*. That giant is a golem—Stop snickering, Thor—Do you know anything about the golem, Jack?"

"I'm here to listen and to learn. Shoot."

"Think back to sixteenth-century Prague. Jews were being accused of murdering Christian babies to grace their Passover dinner plates. Rabbi Yehuda Levi ben Bezalel—"

"Rabbi Loew for short, right, Es?" interjected Ohnstad.

"Right, Thor. At least you've *listened*. The rabbi read the *Sefer Yetzirah*—"

"Es alludes to the kabbalistic sacred book of formation," put in Ohnstad.

"—and heard a mysterious voice telling him how to create a creature out of clay."

"Gypsum is a kind of clay before it hardens, you know, Jack," said Ohnstad.

Esther waved her hands impatiently. "Let me get on with my story. So the Rabbi got his son-in-law and a pupil to fashion a huge human body out of clay on the River Moldavka. They walked around him seven times, chanting a kabbalistic formula, and the clay came to life. He was somewhere in his late thirties, red hot and smiling."

"What'd they do with him?" I asked, though I already knew the story.

"He was protector of Jews against the murderous plots of Christian priests, and he doubled as household servant. He'd perform any task—the rabbi would stick written instructions in his mouth every night. But the golem couldn't speak."

"And he took offense that he was always working and not having fun like the teenagers," added Ohnstad. "Exploited labor! And he didn't like not having a soul and not being fully human."

"Yes, Thor, he got out of hand and got drunk and belligerent. The rabbi decided to put him down and forced his son-in-law to chant the secret formula walking around the golem in the opposite direction. This reduced him to lifeless clay again. But I prefer to think of the golem in his role as preserver and protector—"

"And dishwasher, floor scrubber, cook, personal secretary, and chauffeur."

"We could all use a golem," she replied. "Okay, it's just my hunch. There are some things I simply enjoy believing—no harm done. What I believe is that the Cardiff Giant has been reanimated as a golem and is here to protect Jews. Take it or leave it."

"No evidence against it, must admit," said Ohnstad.

"And *I'd* like to believe it," I said. "But I wasn't aware that Cooperstown has a large Jewish population."

"Not Cooperstown—Sharon Springs, right next door," she said. "I'm doing some family history there. The legend is that my grandfather left an ancient copy of the Zohar in the synagogue of one of those ruined hotels. Zohar—that's another sacred text of the Kabbalah."

"Jews came up from the city to drink the waters and bathe," said Ohnstad. "Whole town reeks of sulfur. Eighty hotels at its peak, turn of the century. Only one open now. Many are still standing but ruined and empty."

"Sounds spooky," I said.

"It is. They filmed *I Drink Your Blood* at the Hotel Roosevelt."

"And sad," said Esther. "All that history is just a bunch of faded photographs now. Jack, would you please pass the *lekhem*—I mean bread. Look, there's a tuxedo cat! This is where Kabbalah comes in handy. We feed her before we feed ourselves—then we perform the *tikkun olam*, passing bread and repairing the broken vessels."

"But we haven't broken any vessels," I noted.

Esther put butter on her fingers, inviting the cat to lick. Not satisfied with fingers, the cat sprang onto the table, clawing and pulling the tablecloth and, sure enough, breaking vessels.

The three of us mopped up Campari and brushed aside glass shards while the cat bolted to the top of an adjacent table, breaking more vessels.

"Oh, not again. Stop that, Reuben!" said the waitress, chasing him away.

"Did she say *Reuben*?" asked Esther. "The cat has a gematria of 259—that's a sacred number."

"Gematria?"

"You know, the numerical equivalent of the Hebrew letters."

"Oh. Of what use?" I asked.

"Lots of uses. You learn how to apply these numbers to everyday life. There are 613 commandments to go with the 613 parts of the soul. It sounds far-fetched, I know, but all of this is explained by Rabbi Isaac Luria."

"He'd better explain his explanation," said Ohnstad.

"Six hundred and thirteen commandments! I have trouble keeping track of ten," I said.

Esther laughed. "It's not so hard once you get the hang of it. The idea is rather lovely. The sacred vessels of the world have been broken ever since Adam's expulsion from Eden. It's the goal of Kabbalah to repair the vessels. That much is simple enough."

"I agree, the world is broken. But where to start?"

"With your own name, Jack. In Hebrew that's *yud aleph gimmel kaf*—or ten plus one plus three plus twenty equals thirty-four. That's a sacred number too, I seem to remember. How old are you?"

"Forty-five."

"Now I'm sure that's a sacred number! It's the numerical value of the Hebrew for *man*—adam." She laughed. "You must be Jewish." As Esther began to take an interest in me, her eyes slightly crossed.

"No, I'm nothing at all. Mongrel mutt from the Midwest."

Ohnstad seemed to be monitoring Esther while she gave me a half-hour kabbalistic primer. He looked by turns amused and quizzical as she spoke on with the enthusiasm of an initiate. Mere hours after arriving in town, I flattered myself to think this might be some weird kind of fix-up. For my part, I was finding Esther unusually appealing for a psychoanalyst, with her black hair done in a louche retro bob, skinny high-waisted torso, and warm, well-tuned voice—like an announcer's for a classical-music station.

Finally I interrupted her. "Do you work Kabbalah into your practice?"

"All along, even before I read Rabbi Luria. I was treating neurosis by restoring all the exiled *kellipots*. My clients were escaping Galut and achieving Geulah. I was doing this all along without knowing it. *Tikkun* is what Freud meant by bringing repressed desires into full consciousness."

"Oh."

Her cell went off again. "Sorry, must take this call . . . Now Howie, that's not what Freud meant by transference . . . please, Howie! . . . Oh go ahead, but I'm holding the cell at arm's length . . ."

We could hear digital wheezes while Esther rolled her eyes. "Okay, Howie, I hope you feel better. But now you must explore what

I was telling you about *noten* and *mekabel* and the tetragrammaton . . . No, I don't consider this a phone session, no charge—but please, I'm having dinner. Take a Klonopin and turn in early. Shalom!"

"Your sister's working at the opera?"

"Half-sister, Sheila—Sheila Drake. Set designer and costumer."

"Great set designer!" Ohnstad said. "But Sheila Drake is a lousy name for an Indian."

Esther explained. "We shared a terrible father, a Christian Science furrier. Sheila's mother's half-Huron—my mother's totally Jewish. I took her name, Federman, and dumped Drake." I silently pondered how many Christian Scientists were furriers. "We both hated our father," she continued. "Every reason to. He tried to keep doctors at bay when I was almost dead from whooping cough, three years old. My mother intervened and I lived. They had a fight over that—seems he was angry I recovered. Then he persuaded her not to check out a lump. He left her and married Sheila's mother a few weeks later, just after my mother was diagnosed with breast cancer."

"You know, Jack," said Ohnstad, "a Christian Scientist doesn't believe in sickness, sin, or death, especially when he's the occasion of them."

"You're clever for a businessman," I said.

"Blame it on Wharton."

"Thor is really smart, take it from Sheila and me, but you may have noticed he's nosy. Watch out!"

"Back to your father," I said, with the sense I was playing therapist to an analyst. "That's an awfully sad story, no joking matter. But may I ask whether you now hate all men?"

She looked me crookedly in the eyes. "I can make exceptions."

Ohnstad pitched forward, and it was hard to tell if he was chortling or choking. I hit him hard on the back and tried to remember the Heimlich maneuver. Reuben must have thought I was attacking an old friend. He hissed as he leapt from an adjoining table, digging claws into my right arm.

Esther raised her voice. *"Khet yud yud mem vav shin mem yud shin!"*

She explained that this was what you say to ward off afflictions caused by pets. It seemed to work, for Reuben withdrew his claws. The waitress gave me a paper towel to staunch the flow, and Ohnstad caught his breath.

While Esther took a call from another suicidal client, Ohnstad proposed dropping in on a rehearsal at Glimmerglass Opera to meet Sheila.

An hour later he drove us to the Otesaga. "See you kids later."

"What room are you in?" asked Esther.

"227."

"Jack, that's the kabbalistic number for *male*. And I'm in 157, the number for *female*."

She squeezed my hand as we walked through the lobby and up the staircase.

"My room or yours?" I asked.

"We must have sex in both rooms for balance, the middle column of *Sefirot*, we horses of fire. Three times, if you are able."

— Chapter Four —

BACKSTAGE

Having sex according to a kabbalistic script required such a mishmash of sacred postures, rituals, numerology, and Hebraic alphabetical chants that all I could manage was the sacred number of one. Happily, Esther didn't insist on more, and we parted on friendly terms in the morning. I agreed to accompany her to Sharon Springs the following week.

That afternoon Ohnstad picked me up in his BMW. He had bought the old Busch Mansion and stayed at the Hotel Otesaga only when he passed out. We began the drive along Otsego Lake, eight miles to the Glimmerglass Opera, where the world premiere of *The Last of the Mohicans* was in rehearsal. When we passed Three-Mile Point, Ohnstad began a not-so-subtle interrogation.

"You and Esther seemed to hit it off last night."

"She's quite the enthusiast. Thanks for the intro. But I should have been taking notes. For the life of me I can't remember which gematria is which."

"You had the right number, sport. Guess I should tell you that's how she's been screening men."

"Oh?"

"Afraid so. She was here three years ago visiting her sister. To tell you the truth, I took a fancy for a brief spell. But the gematria for *Thor Ohnstad* didn't add up. And I was staying in the wrong room."

"Too bad. Booking the right room should have been easy—you own the hotel."

He didn't seem to find this funny. "Esther's quite a dish. But—well, you'll see. There's no one like Sheila."

We passed the Busch Mansion on our left. "That's my house," he said. "Not bad for a working-class kid from St. Paul. Built in 1901 by a hops czar. Colonial Revival and Queen Anne & Shingle. Used to be called Uncas Lodge. Owned by the Busch family till I bought them out last year. I'll be giving a party—you can meet the top crust of Cooperstown."

"You sound more and more like Jay Gatsby," I said. "I thought I was walking into a novel by James Fenimore Cooper."

"Never read *Gatsby*, never even read *Last of the Mohicans*. No time for novels."

We passed the Mohican Sunken Wreck to our right and then Sunken Island, where they shot a scene for the 1911 film adaptation of *The Deerslayer*. It was visited daily by the *Chief Uncas*, a sturdy mahogany excursion boat built in 1912 by August Busch. Even the steam whistle still worked. Then to the Glimmerglass opera house, a flimsy, non-insulated concoction with gray aluminum siding, once likened to an overachieving Quonset hut. Here, every summer, some of the world's best operatic performances took place. The audience came from the world over, but locals stayed away, preferring auto demolition derbies at the Otsego County Fair.

Backstage we found Sheila engaged in an altercation with Hazel Bouche, the famed mezzo singing the role of Cora, the wise but doomed mulatto of Cooper's tragic tale.

"Sorry, Miss what's-your-name, but I cannot wear black this month," said Hazel Bouche. "Pluto is out of alignment with Mercury, and Venus is in retrograde. I'm informing the orchestra that the rehearsal must be postponed until four o'clock, when Venus and the moon are no longer at right angles. Today I'm advised to have my own way in all matters. Are you listening? It's for the good of the production."

I already knew lots about this diva through feature articles in the *Times Sunday Magazine* and elsewhere, but had never eyeballed her. The role of Cora was appropriate. Of mixed race from the nation's capital, Hazel Bouche identified with her Haitian roots. She got her big break in her early twenties by successfully sticking voodoo pins into an effigy of the diva for whom she was bench-warming in a production of *Carmen* at the Kennedy Center. Nancy Reagan turned her on to horoscopes and psychics, to which she herself added palmistry, the tarot, and born-again Christianity. Well-divorced three times and now forty, she had residences in Milan, Manhattan, and Port-au-Prince.

She looked the part of Cora, of whom Cooper wrote, "The tresses of this lady were shining and black, like the plumage of the raven. Her complexion was not brown, but it appeared charged with the color of rich blood that seemed ready to burst its bounds." Hazel Bouche burst bounds mostly by venting spleen on subordinates.

Sheila stood her ground. "But Miss Bouche, you must wear the black-beaded sash. You are the tragic figure, and it's part of the plot line. Everybody alludes to your black apparel."

"Silence, child. I cannot and will not wear black! Royal purple is the only color for an Aries when Mars is in the orbit of Venus."

"But Miss Bouche, Cora is hardly royalty," said Sheila. "She's just an army brat!"

"Army brat? Where's the production manager? I'll have you dismissed *out of hand*."

Ohnstad intervened. "Miss Bouche, I'm not the production manager but, as you must know, I am this company's principal benefactor. Sheila Drake is a preeminent designer. Might I suggest a compromise?"

"What about blackish purple?" I put in. "Or purplish black?"

"Okay by me," said Sheila, relenting.

The diva's heaving bosom calmed somewhat at our diplomatic proposal. When she marched off to the makeup room, Sheila, Thor, and I conversed. We were surrounded by Sheila's scenic flats that projected powerfully the great forest of the Mohicans.

"Esther says you are part Huron."

"One-quarter. But in a prior life I was one hundred percent. Working on this opera is like coming home. I have déjà vu moments every day." She stared at her flats like an old stamping ground. "You're here because of the Cardiff Giant?"

"Yes. Do you have a theory?"

"Well, since you asked, yes. I believe the giant was carved thousands of years ago by Druids. Like the menhirs and dolmens of Stonehenge. The Druids have simply returned to claim their own."

Ohnstad sighed. "Must admit, no evidence against it."

I thought it better not to choose in this matter of golems or Druids. Taking a quick inventory of Sheila, I couldn't see much Huron in her. She looked more Irish than Indian. Like Esther, she spoke with animation and gusto, yet I sensed more vulnerability. Her long auburn hair was a jumble, her body hard to guess at because of baggy trousers, and her large green heavy-lidded eyes not unlike those of a Bassett hound. I felt a twinge that Esther hadn't inspired.

"These sets are terrific," I said. "You've out-Coopered Cooper."

"Thanks. I have to admit, you're looking at my best work. It's sort of a convergence—everything I've done has been leading up to this. That's why I was defying the diva, not my usual style. Divas think everybody else is in the service industry. Usually I let them think I know my place."

"Know your place?" interjected Ohnstad. He looked perplexed. "You're pretty adept at letting others know *their* place, or where their place is *not!*"

She looked at him askance as if to say, *Shut your trap.* To me, "Thor doesn't know what he's talking about."

Again I thought it best to change the subject. "The trees and plants in these sets are so intense. Where do you get your inspiration?"

"Thor makes fun of me, but I've been taking adult seminars in Plant Spirit Medicine. Every plant has a spirit of its own—you just have to intuit it, speak to it. When I did these sets, I felt the painted trees and plants were speaking to me and thanking me for bringing them to life."

Thor shuffled toward the set, as if he needed a moment for recovery, turned to us and said, "It's just one feature of her complex personality, Jack. Sheila subscribes to many New Age notions. Let's see if I've got them all—vibrational healing, channeling, rebirthing, pyramids, alchemy, astrology, Zen Buddhism, auras, multiple chemical sensitivity, shamanism, psychics, I Ching, vegetarianism, and not drinking water with food. Did I get them all, pet?"

"Dowsing, you left out dowsing. Thor thinks everything boils down to money and matter in motion. Esther and I try to convince him there must be something more out there and in here." She pointed to her heart. "*In here!*"

"Plant Spirit Medicine, what's that?" I asked.

"Better than telling you, let me show you sometime, Jack. I've got a day off next week after the opening. Let's all go on a hike. I'll introduce you to some plants."

"Great idea," said Ohnstad, "but just the two of you. No time for botany. I've got money to make."

Chapter Five

TO THE KINGFISHER CASTLE

Next morning, recovering from another night of complex kabbalistic sex during which I managed to achieve the sacred number of three, I got a call from Tarbox. He had intercepted on his sheriff's cell phone a message sent from one alien spaceship to another. These aliens had already mastered the English language, for they had no discernible accent. They spoke of "colonizing" humans and had set up a laboratory to that end in Kingfisher Castle.

"That could explain the strange lights coming from the turret," I offered.

"Yeah, this is our big chance. Me and the posse are gonna catch 'em in our nets 'fore anybody else gets abducted. Thought you'd like ter come along, cover it for the press. I'm available for an interview and photo op."

"What are you going to do with these aliens once you've caught them?"

"Me and the posse disagree on that. I say we exhibit 'em at the fair. They say we sell 'em ter Steven Spielberg. We agree they gotta force the Cardiff Giant ter stop having sex with our women and return 'im ter the Farmers' Museum. We'll need to feed 'em sumpin, so we're bringing frankfurters and sauerkraut."

"Good thinking," I said.

That evening, after sunset, I met with Tarbox and his posse of locals at the Otsego County Jail on Main Street—a charming Second Empire edifice with copula, mansard roof, dormers, molding, and trimmed white-shuttered windows. Tarbox didn't fit here.

The volunteers were from the Local Alien Abduction Focus Group, the LAAFG. They carried large nylon nets attached to modified fishing rods. We embarked on the *Chief Uncas* with lights out and engine turned low until we were about one-eighth of a nautical mile away. Then Tarbox turned off the engine and silently we cut through the water to the small estuary where the castle stood, looking spooky in the moonlight.

"Sure enough," whispered Snodgrass, second lieutenant of the posse. "Lights in the turret. Dem's aliens!"

They had been watching official police videos of swat teams but had all the coordination of the Keystone Cops. As an embedded reporter, I was carrying a video camera but hardly knew where to point it. Everyone had a different notion of which way to go. One tripped on his own net as he leapt off the *Uncas*, another fell headfirst into the water, two collided as they rounded the turret from opposite directions. Tarbox approached the entrance with an old boom box. He started blaring the coded electronic tones of *Close Encounters of the Third Kind*.

We made our way up the winding staircase. I admit I was nervous about the outcome but well, next to an evening of miniature golf in Muncie, this was high adventure. We could hear the muffled sounds of surprised aliens speaking what sounded like the local upstate dialect.

"Who the Sam Hill are you?" one of them shouted from above. "Friends or foes?"

Tarbox led the charge into the upper chamber with Snodgrass and the rest of the posse flailing nets toward a group of six aliens with surprisingly hominid features—to the extent one could make them out in the dim light cast by lanterns. And the lanterns themselves were surprisingly low-tech for aliens, the sort you might pick up at a Kmart.

There were shouts and screams. "Get that one," ordered Tarbox, mistaking a member of his own posse for an alien. The nets flew this way and that until the whole posse was wrapped up in its own nets. The aliens were standing about, looking down quietly at wriggling humans and scratching what looked like ordinary craniums. I was free of nets and continued recording.

One of the aliens approached Tarbox, entangled in nylon and helpless.

"Say, aren't you that pig farmer Barry Tarbox?"

"County sheriff," he snorted. "Now why don't yah help me out of dis here net and let's strike a deal. You tell the Cardiff Giant ter stop having sex with our women and yah stop colonizing us. Obvious yer aliens 'cause yah look just like us—in fact, you there, yah look exactly like Sam Fuller from Herkimer College. You couldn't pull dat off without advanced pod technology. Sign this form!" He pushed a piece of paper through the mesh. "We'll give yah some sauerkraut and yah go back ter the Andromeda galaxy. No shit."

"But shit's what it's all about, Sheriff Tarbox."

"Huh?"

"Did you say *colonizing*?"

"Yeah, I intercepted yer messages."

By now our eyes had adjusted to the dim light. Sam Fuller, the respectably dressed spokesman for the aliens, seemed to have a eureka moment. He was quite articulate for a community-college instructor in remedial English.

"I think there's been a mistake. This is as embarrassing for us as it is for you. You there with the video, kindly shut it down."

I complied.

"I hate to disappoint," continued Sam, "but we're not alien colonizers. We're the Local High Colonics Recovery Focus Group, the LHCRFG. *Colonics*, not *colonizing*, Sheriff Tarbox. To be a member, you've got to show proof of hospitalization."

"For what?" I asked.

"I suffered electrolyte depletion," said one group member.

"I got my colon perforated and caught septicemia."

"I came down with amebic dysentery."

"It turned me into a homosexual," said another.

I knew something about colonic irrigation but had no idea there were high colonics recovery focus groups. "Why are you holed up in this castle?" I asked. By now Tarbox and the other trapped members of the posse were beginning to take Fuller seriously.

"Good question. Well, the best light I can cast on it is this: We feel a collective shame at having permitted twenty or more gallons of water containing herbs, enzymes, wheat grass extract, and harmful bacteria to be inserted into our rectums by technicians who didn't know their own asses from holes in the ground. For the past two years we've gathered here and there in dark private places to talk it through. *Dark* because we can still hardly look one another in the eyes. *Private* because we're afraid of being bugged. This castle is the ideal place. No electrical outlets. No frills. I guess you could say it's a self-punishing environment . . . just what we need."

"Barry," said Snodgrass, "this makes sense to me. Why don't we just bugger off and leave 'em alone?"

"We'll let you out of your nets on one condition," said Sam. "You must keep this to yourselves. The last thing we seek is publicity. We've got a full membership already and a waiting list. We can't take any more applicants. Meanwhile, we'll clear out of this castle. There's a rusted mobile home full of muskrats on Gulf Road that will do just as well."

Sailing back on the *Chief Uncas*, I asked Tarbox if he still wished to sit for an interview and photo op. He blinked and grunted, his dreams of glory at the Otsego County Fair now deferred at best.

"Let's just say this was a trial run. The giant's still at bay. Probably more abductions goin' on. Me and the posse stand firm. We're goin' ter take back Otsego County. Cain't you see? We just need a little more practice with our nets!"

— *Chapter Six* —

A NIGHT AT THE OPERA

Tabby: "Tabby and Harris here once again, coming to you live from Cooperstown, New York, home of the Cardiff Giant. Lots has been going on here for your Thursday morning Cream of Wheat. We've just received an exclusive report that Kingfisher Castle was scene of a caper last night involving colonizing aliens and members of the Local Alien Abduction Focus Group, the LAAFG. But nobody's talking. We're fortunate to have with us an alien abduction expert, Dr. Albert Ockham of New York University. Why, Dr. Ockham, are group members denying this caper took place?"

Dr. Ockham: "I've spoken with group leadership. They are denying that they are in denial, which can mean only one thing—they are in denial. To their credit, it could well be that denial of denial has been pre-programmed through digital chips implanted against their will by the aliens. No one has yet stepped forward to deny neck-chip implants. I conclude that something very strange happened last night at Kingfisher Castle. Certainly there's no denying there's no evidence against it."

Harris: "We invite our viewers to cast a vote on the question, *Did members of the LAAFG confront colonizing aliens last night at Kingfisher Castle?* Results later in the show."

Tabby: "Now then, for what's coming up in Cooperstown for your Thursday evening happy hour. It's the gala opening of the

Glimmerglass Opera and many celebs will be there. Hazel Bouche will sing the role of Cora in *Last of the Mohicans* and Martial Gaudi will be singing Natty Bumppo. There are rumors of a sizzling romance between these operatic superstars—rumors we can neither confirm nor deny. But do take note that neither superstar is denying the rumors. The opera is based on a true story by James Fenimore Cooper, a local."

In room 227 of the Otesaga, Esther and I laughed our way through the coanchors' drivel. "I thought they fired anchors when they reach a certain age—the women at least," said Esther, on her second helping of whitefish. "Tabby's bouffant dates her. She thinks she's Jackie O. Those Chiclets hurt my eyes."

"So snarky, Esther," I said. "What's your take on Harris?"

"Have you been to the Bronx Zoo? He looks like a warthog."

"So my competition is a crone and a warthog. Maybe I don't need to work so hard."

"They want us to cast a vote. Shall I call in a 'yes'?"

"Do it. Sheriff Tarbox needs a plurality."

I left Esther in bed munching on toasted challah and closed the bathroom door behind me. I observed myself nude in the bathroom mirror. This isn't something I often do, deeming my physical person a tagalong that requests minimal upkeep and the occasional gifts of chocolate and fresh air. Not quite six feet tall and fairly slender, I've received the occasional compliment, gratifying to someone who never works out. But I have asymmetrical features that emerged from an indiscriminate Midwest gene pool of English, German, Scotch-Irish, and the unscrubbed peasantry betrayed by my surname Thrasher. Not enough of a narcissist, you might say. I got up the courage to make an inventory. My rear end bore baseball bat bruises, my right arm displayed Reuben's murderous gouges, my upper torso boasted scratches and hickeys inflicted by rough kabbalistic sex, and my legs had suffered abrasions by teeth and elbows at Kingfisher Castle.

"At this rate I'll be hamburger in a week," I said through the door.

"Kosher hamburger," replied Esther. "You know, Jack, our *zivvug* was much improved last night. We're not even *partzufim* but you aroused my *mayim nukvim*."

I was a quick study and knew what she was talking about: Our coupling was in the same league with the supernals and I stirred her female waters.

"You are some *nukva*," I replied. Frankly, my improved performance was owing to fantasies about my upcoming initiation into Plant Spirit Medicine, whose priestess seemed to have a more direct line to my *yesod*—or *zayin*, if you'd rather. I must say that Esther's application of Kabbalah to everyday life seemed much more literal and numerological than the Kabbalah we find in Lawrence Durrell's novel *Balthazar*, where this esoteric Jewish religion is enmeshed in spiritual mystery and ennobling. The great scholar Gershom Scholem established the central role of mysticism in Judaism. Doesn't everybody know this much? But I was willing to play along with Esther for the nonce, since one rarely encounters the Kabbalah of Everyday Life in Muncie, Indiana. And there was no hint of suffocating piety in this adventurous woman.

That night, Thor, Esther, and I drove to the opera house for the gala opening. On the exterior balcony a brass ensemble blared Copland's "Fanfare for the Common Man."

"That damn noise is triggering a migraine," said Thor, rubbing his temples. We sat in the benefactors' row next to Bittner, the composer, and awaited the curtain.

Yes, we waited. And waited. 8:20. 8:30. 8:45 p.m. The audience began to get impatient and thumped feet on the floor, shaking the entire aluminum box. Finally, over the sound system came an explanation. "We regret the delay. Miss Bouche begs to inform you that, being an Aries, she will be unable to sing the role of Cora until Mars is in declination to the orbit of Uranus. Happily, her attendant astrologer tells her that this will happen at exactly nine thirteen Eastern Standard Time. Until then we suggest you review the synopsis to be found in your programs."

This announcement wasn't well received. The booing and hissing of nine hundred spectators was unseemly but every bit as understandable as the communality of feeling that attends a lynching. Holding his head in agony at the clamor, Ohnstad shuffled up the aisle and out. Esther and I joined in the stomping and shouting. The uproar was all the more remarkable because the median age of this audience was roughly eighty.

At 9:13 p.m., the curtain rose and Cooper's story as revamped by Bittner began to unfold. Sheila's powerful sets and costumes quelled the mob for a time. Here were trees that looked like tortured giants, shaped boulders to rival Stonehenge, and a great waterfall worthy of Hudson River Valley painters. *The Last of the Mohicans* is, as you know, a story of miscegenation. The bad Indian, Magua, abducts and tries to seduce Cora—of mixed blood herself, so why all the fuss? Hazel Bouche seemed in good form and the audience was ready to forgive. Sitting next to Bittner, though, I noticed the composer flinched whenever Cora took center stage.

"What's the matter?" I whispered.

"She's shifting keys and getting the words all wrong!"

As the opera wore on, the other performers seemed taken aback whenever they sang alongside Cora. Bumppo, Chingachgook, Alice, Tamenund, Uncas, and Magua began stumbling and losing their way. Bittner pulled his hair, seeming to lift himself out of his seat. "She's changing everything!" he seethed.

When the time came for doomed Cora to beg the Delaware chieftain for her freedom from the rapacious Magua, the conductor laid down his baton. Over the sound system came the announcement: "Miss Bouche informs management that, owing to the recent declination of Mars relative to the orbit of Uranus, as it were, she will be unable to die this evening. Instead she will be treating us all to a happy ending. Since Cora will not be killed, Uncas and Magua have no reason to die either. In light of these last-minute changes, the orchestra is substituting the wedding march from *The Marriage of Figaro* for the tragic aria to have been sung by Cora and Natty

Bumppo. Instead of dying at the hands of a Huron, Cora will be marrying Uncas." Uncas was the good Indian.

There was loud booing at this fortunate turn of events. Bittner pitched forward in a faint and was taken out on a stretcher. But I must say that Mozart's wedding march was worth a lifetime of cacophony by Bittner.

Just as the curtain calls began, there was such a round of thunderclaps that Hazel Bouche, beaming through her elaborate curtseys, apparently misheard the boos as bravos—in a final triumph of astrology over all.

— *Chapter Seven* —

THE STORM

Having survived a night at the opera, patrons staggered to the reception tent for champagne. Sheila emerged from backstage in a funk, no wonder. I accompanied her and Esther to the reception, glad to be in the company of both women without Thor looking over my shoulder.

The thunderclaps were getting louder and distant lightning more intense, but this performance of *Mohicans* had put mere natural calamity into perspective. Everybody drank champagne and refrained from throwing rotten fruit at the cast.

As the champagne went to my head, I tried my hand at flirtation. "Sheila, the Huron are the bad guys in Cooper's novel. May I ask— are you bad too?"

She paused at the fatuity of my question. Then, "Hasn't Thor told you I'm celibate? . . . I used to be bad enough."

"That's for sure," said Esther. "Sheila's a reformed strumpet."

Silence. Sheila didn't find this funny.

"I hope you're not a zealot on the issue, Sheila," I said jauntily. "Do you mind if others carry on in the usual manner?"

Sheila caught Esther and me glancing at one another and knew enough about her half-sister to draw a conclusion. "No, Sodomites, carry on without me. Three's a crowd." I flattered myself to hear a flirtatious undertone in this.

"Well, Sheila, what did you think of the performance?" Not a tactful question.

"I'm afraid Hazel Bouche has given the horoscope a black eye," Esther put in. "Isn't astrology on your own list of New Age fixes, sis?"

To my mind Esther's literal-minded version of Kabbalah exceeded even horoscopes in divinatory presumption. I held my tongue.

"Low down on it, actually. Too abstract. Plant Spirit Medicine is the path. Remember our date, Jack."

I swelled at the idea that the sisters were tugging at me, engaged in some sort of rivalry. Yes, my fortunes they were a-changin'.

"How long have you two known Thor Ohnstad?"

Silence.

"I find him diverting for a businessman," I began, "but I've been getting a larger dose than I bargained for."

Silence. Esther looked at Sheila as if to say, *You go first.* Sheila looked at Esther as if to say, *Keep your damn mouth shut.*

The silence was broken by a thunderclap so powerful that two hundred inebriated patrons were jolted to attention. Then came the downpour, trapping everybody and turning the tent into a giant drum. We huddled toward the center while I engaged in nervous small talk about tornados. I felt an erotic surge when, amid thunder, Sheila was forced to monitor my lips.

Suddenly from the perimeter of the crowd, the diva's scream broke champagne goblets. Natty Bumppo bellowed, "It's the Cardiff Giant!"

Through rain I could barely make out the frame of a gigantic figure slowly slouching in our direction, easily ten feet tall. Never did two hundred patrons so quickly disperse into a maelstrom. Esther seemed to forget that the giant was the golem who wouldn't hurt a fly, and Sheila forgot he was a mystical Druidic sculpture. We ran with the rest of them. Looking back I could make out the gray stone face of the giant as he leaned against a tent pole. He could have passed for Frankenstein's monster pathetically crying out, "Friend!

Friend!"—except that he was smiling. Was he taking some pleasure in crashing this party? Who knew? But one thing I knew for sure was that I now had a story for my producers.

The next day they agreed to extend my stay at the Otesaga but were quite firm about my getting some footage of the giant. Otherwise, they would resort to digital imaging, a more costly way of getting at the truth of things.

— Part Two —

BREAK ON THROUGH

— *Chapter Eight* —

TO SHARON SPRINGS

"Route 28 is not the way to Sharon Springs," I insisted.

"Let's take it anyway—28 is a perfect number," said Esther with warmth, revving the engine. "There are only five others."

"Let me guess—3, 7, 11, 69, 96?"

"Not even close, Jack: 6, 28; then 496; then 8,128; then 33,550,336; then 8,589,869,056."

"I should have known. Well, must be something to Kabbalah. Route 8,589,869,056 is coming up—next right."

"Can't fool me, mister. That's Route 20."

"Okay, but it goes straight to Sharon Springs. Isn't 20 a sacred number?" I was going on a hunch that most numbers are sacred for one reason or another.

"Sacred, yes, perfect no. How many times must I explain the difference? We need perfect."

After driving forty miles out of our way on Route 28 and raising our velocity periodically to conform to various sacred numbers on the speedometer, Esther raced the rental Mercedes down Main Street, ran an intersection, and slid half-circle to a stop near the entrance to the Adler Hotel.

The doorman leapt backward. "Lady, why stop there? Just break on through to the registration desk."

"We're here, Jack. Let's get to work."

I was relieved at the prospect of searching for a sacred kabbalistic tome, figuring we'd be rummaging safely on foot.

The Adler had a built-in synagogue and sulfur bath, offering a special package of six baths, four massages, one hot pack, and one Scotch douche—all for $185. Esther insisted we instead visit the Imperial Baths down the street—older and more sulfurous. Sharon Springs's ubiquitous stench was sufficient in itself to account for the village's decline—the enigma was how it ever got started.

Beyond the superintendent of Bath's box office, there were three dour Hassidim whose sole function was the slow inspection of tickets. Esther ascertained, speaking fluent Hebrew, that we were their first customers in six months.

We were ushered into the Vapor Room, at whose center stood a large many-tiered Victorian fountain, flanked by four naked light bulbs hanging from the ceiling. Moss covered phlegm-green walls. Another squad of Hassidim was at the ready, handing us small towels, threadbare but rich in discoloration.

"Not to worry," said Esther, "we won't undress. A naked woman would make the Hassidim faint. We're just doing inhalations. People used to come here to cure lung infections—breathe the sulfur."

"But I don't have a lung infection."

"Don't be so unteachable. Remember, each of your organs represents a different vocalization of the tetragrammaton, the Word of God. Try to grasp what I'm telling you about lungs. The letter *heh* is the sole letter in the Hebrew alphabet that requires no oral movement. The Talmud teaches that *heh* is the aboriginal breath, the source of all creative power. When you say *heh* you massage—"

Here the Hassidim turned on the fountain and water started cascading down its tiers, sending out orange mist that quickly enveloped us as we sat on clammy vinyl lounge chairs, purchased on the cheap, I'd guess, at local garage sales.

"—you mass-saahaage your lungs and re-cre-eeate the mo-ho-ment of your bir-hirth . . ."

Esther and I began heaving with paroxysms. "Is this suppo-hosed to ha-haa-p-pppen?" I wheezed. These sulfurous inhalations were making Tarbox's pig farm ambrosial by comparison.

"Yes, it's a spiritual exercise, not meant to be ea-hea-heasy." Esther was gasping like an expensive copper kettle. "We achieve balance and find the *Zoh-ha-ar-ar*. A spiritual qu-qu-qu-quest"—At this point Esther coughed so hard her lounge chair collapsed. She lay on the slick fungal floor—"requires a spiritually refi-fi-hined seeker."

Amid my own bronchospasms I detected that the Hassidim had ceased to be dour and even evinced slight smiles as they watched their therapy go to work. They themselves didn't make a sound until some survival instinct got the better of Esther, and we bolted for the escape corridor. Our hosts then coughed to hint a gratuity was in order.

I tipped enormously, fearing we'd otherwise be locked in and perish.

"Okay, Ja-aa-ack-ack-ack, I admit—that was a bit mu-u-u-uch." Our spasms didn't relent, so Esther said we must take the waters down the block at the Magnesia Temple, an 1860 Renaissance Revival structure with Corinthian columns. At the center were twin stone lion heads from which spouted the highly esteemed magnesia water, said to cure everything from gout and impotence to depression and female troubles. If you were suffering from an overdose of medicinal waters, the best cure, it seemed, was homeopathic—more waters.

Sure enough, the spasms subsided after we'd quaffed some of the smelly stuff, a liquid not unlike Mr. Plumber.

We dined at the Adler.

"Okay, Esther, give me a refresher—what are we looking for and why?"

"You have a dim memory for a reporter." It was in fact my way of checking for consistency. "It's like this," she said as we ladled up the borsht Romanoff and munched on challah. "I'm not that hard to analyze. You've surmised I hate my father. You're right. His part of my genome feels like a contaminant."

"So you're seeking Jewish roots to purge your father?"

"Right. Took my mother's name—remember, I dumped *Drake* for *Federman*. Her father, my grandfather, was a Polish Jew in the rag trade, working out of Rockaway. He hit on the idea of selling used clothes to Africa—simply a matter of fumigating them stateside and having them laundered in West Africa. They sold as prestige items in outdoor markets. He made a fortune." We set at the potato knishes and prepared for the brisket.

"As I recall, his son-in-law, the, uh, furrier, did your mother out of her share?"

"Yes, her marriage to a goy made my grandfather wonder about her. He'd say, 'If she could be with him, how good she could be altogether?' He favored his two sons—my knuckle-headed uncles—but didn't disinherit her. My father managed to abscond with her money and desert her at death's door. Another reason for hating him. But hatred de-energizes my *nefesh*."

"*Nefesh*, yes, the animal life in you."

"You're learning, Jack. Better to purge this father altogether. I want to bond with my dead mother and grandfather."

"Sounds like an improvement on Freud."

She ignored this as we chewed the tough flesh. "Strong memories of my mother—in an alcove, no windows, the waves outside, the cancer taking over. I get my own boobs checked every three months. Her parents outlived her—I remember them sitting shivah, quietly weeping on the cardboard. In happier days they came out here summers and stayed at the Hadassah Arms and took the waters."

"Very affecting. But what's this about the Zohar in one of the old hotels? Are we caught up in some variation on *Name of the Rose*?"

"Good analogy. My grandfather was no kabbalist but in one of his visits to Sharon Springs shortly after my mother died, he came across a rare old edition of the Zohar in the synagogue at the Hadassah Arms. Maybe because Kabbalah is beyond the pale for most Jews, the volume was tucked sideways behind Funk and Wagnall's twelve-volume *Jewish Encyclopedia*. My grandfather was checking to see if there was an entry on the medieval rag trade when he spotted the hidden Zohar and pulled out the entire encyclopedia to get at it. Well, all the dust triggered an asthma attack. He lugged the Zohar to the hotel porch to catch his breath. It had oddly gathered no dust and seemed to quiver alive in his hands."

"Sounds talismanic."

"Lots of evidence it was, Jack. It had powers. My grandfather's lungs cleared right away. He didn't even have to read it—Aramaic wasn't his strong suit. It had a healing aura—and when he took it to his room that night he swore it glowed in the dark. A few people going back to the nineteenth century had signed it on the frontispiece—so he added his own name, Mordechai Federman." She looked up at me, her eyes slightly crossing. "I want to find that signature and add my own."

"For good luck?"

"Yes, and for connection."

"But why do you think it's still in that hotel?"

"The Hadassah Arms was boarded up overnight in 1946 by the state health department when plague-carrying fleas were found in the lobby. Four guests died all at once. The owner had time only to remove valuables from the safe and didn't bother with the synagogue library. He'd inherited the hotel from a distant cousin and didn't know what a treasure he had under his nose. Nobody except my grandfather even knew the existence of the Zohar. He had put it back where he found it and kept quiet. Well, the hotel stayed under quarantine so long the owner went bankrupt and the place never reopened. It's been falling into ruin ever since. The local building inspector denied my petition to search. Said the building could collapse any minute. We need to figure a way to break in tonight and find that book, take it with us."

"And maybe the plague to boot?"

"No chance. Those fleas haven't had any blood to suck for decades."

By now it was dark and we set off from the Adler and walked past the various edifices and ghosts of edifices on Main Street, lit up eerily by the half moon. The Sanatorium Hotel, Sticht's drugstore, the

Imperial Baths, the White Sulfur Temple. To our right beyond Brimstone Creek we could see the Eye Water Spring, the Magnesia Temple, and the Schaefer residence. All these were like memorials to themselves, the vestiges of human hopes and vacation leisure in a ghost town. At South Street we turned right and decided it was time to creep like bandits as we approached the intersection with Center Street. Here stood the Hadassah Arms, built in the 1920s, four stories with gabled dormers. The wraparound porch of Romanesque stone arcades was sagging disconcertingly.

We approached the front door. To the right I could make out a weathered sign with faint letters: Music. Entertainment. Hotel Guests Only. Next to this was a sign of more recent vintage: No Trespassing.

Esther whispered, "This is the very porch where my grandfather sat with the Zohar in his lap." Well okay. Now what? The windows were all boarded up with plywood.

Esther took out a Swiss Army knife with an official miniature crowbar attachment and said, "Jack, remove the plywood."

I set to and in a few minutes had cleared a way to the window, which opened with surprising ease. We peered in using pocket flashlights and beheld a ghastly mélange of rotting overstuffed furniture, cobwebs, tarnished candelabra, and stars of David. Esther had recovered architectural floor plans and knew the whereabouts of the synagogue. We crept through the vestibule and down a creepy corridor. I began to feel stomach pangs I took to be nerves.

"We're there," said Esther, pushing open a door that creaked much like the one in the old radio show *Inner Sanctum*. We cast about with our flashlights. To our right were the bema and an ark with a Torah scroll, and to our left the dust-laden bookshelves. We approached these and quickly checked titles: *Israel's Settlement in Canaan*, *The Pharisees and Their Teachings*, *A History of the Jews in Russia and Poland*, *Old European Jewries*, and many Hebrew titles.

"Here it is," she said. "The *Jewish Encyclopedia*!"

There was—or was I hallucinating?—a faint glow behind the multivolume set. We pulled out the encyclopedia tome by tome and beheld the large leather-bound volume behind, set sideways, its cover suitably ornate for this famous fake.

Fake? Yes, the Zohar was an inspired fake, acknowledged so even by the many scholars who read it devotionally. Journalists must be quick studies. In recent days I'd been reading about the Zohar in essays posted on the internet, where they could readily be plagiarized by students of religion. But I didn't dare confess to Esther that I now knew almost as much about the Zohar as she did.

Here's the story. Moses de Léon was a thirteenth-century Spanish Jewish mystic in need of a living. He began distributing copies of passages he claimed were taken from a massive manuscript composed by a second-century Israelite, Rabbi Shim'on son of Yohai, who spent his life in a cave. These passages were inspired commentary on the first five books of the Bible, the Torah, which the good Rabbi took to be a mystical text written in code.

Moses explained to his wife that nobody "would pay attention to [his] words, and they would pay nothing for them" if it were revealed that he made the whole goddam thing up. "Now that they hear that I am copying from *The Book of Zohar* composed by Rabbi Shim'on son of Yohai through the Holy Spirit, they buy these words at a high price, as you see with your very eyes!" When Moses de Léon died, his widow blew his cover. "Thus and more may God do to me if my husband ever possessed such a book! He wrote it entirely from his own head!"

So Moses de Léon heads the list of great literary fakers— MacPherson, Chatterton, Wise, Irving. But devotees tell us this doesn't impair the inspired nature of the Zohar. After all, eight centuries is pretty ancient too, if not quite so ancient as nineteen centuries.

What Esther and I were looking at was an oversized sixteenth-century Italian edition with finely tooled binding that had somehow ended up in this resort hotel. We hauled it over to the bema and opened the cover. Names, all male, with dates beginning in the late nineteenth century were inscribed on the frontispiece: *Jeremiah Kandelcukier, Hoboken, New Jersey, 1879; Levi Einhorn, Bronx, New*

York, 1899; Malachi Rabinowitz, Borough of Queens, 1904; Motl Szczupakiewicz, Orchard Street, 1910; and many others up to *Mordechai Federman, Rockaway, August 12, 1946.*

"That's my grandfather!" exclaimed Esther. "Jack, we did it! Let's take it out of here."

This was no easy matter with a tome that would make Janson's *History of Art* feel like a dime novel. We clumsily hoisted it and started to depart the synagogue. Then it happened.

Throughout our act of stealth I'd been hearing some faint thumps I took to be raccoons or squirrels. But as we made our way toward the synagogue door, the thumps got louder. So loud they seemed like a large bear or even an elephant—but there had been few reports of bears and none of elephants in Schoharie County. Esther and I exchanged glances and peeked apprehensively out the door.

Coming down the corridor from the direction opposite to what we'd traversed, now at a distance of perhaps sixty feet, was a gigantic form—not a bear, not an elephant, but the Cardiff Giant!

I pointed my flashlight at him and saw the curious stony smile as he continued his slow steady stride in our direction. "Grrrrrrrr!"—a low malevolent growl coming from the depths of reanimated gypsum.

Esther shrieked as we dropped the Zohar and set off down the corridor. Protector and domestic helper? Some golem. We could feel the entire edifice tremble rhythmically as he stalked us. I feared a building collapse. We jumped through the window and headed down the steep lawn.

Whereupon we were ambushed by Schoharie County's counterpart to Barry Tarbox and his men. "You're under arrest for trespassing. Horace, read them their rights!"

"But the Cardiff Giant's in there. He's trespassing too and he's a much bigger fish," I said, relieved at being arrested and spared sudden death at the hands of a malevolent giant.

Horace crept up to peer through the window but saw nothing. "Sure, sure, buddy. The Cardiff Giant's in there and I'm the Jolly *Green* Giant. Tell it to the judge."

There had been so many recent area sightings of the Cardiff Giant that law enforcement had become blasé, not responding to many 911 calls.

Esther and I were handcuffed, put in the backseat of one of two police cars, and taken to Sharon Springs's night court, which hadn't seen any action for six months. The magistrate was cheered to have two customers and set bail at $50,000. Mastercard, Visa, and American Express all turned us down—further proof of our criminal status—so off we went to the county jail, right next to the most sulfurous Stygian pit in the entire county. Because this jail was a modest two-celler, Esther and I could converse through bars, holding our noses.

"Well, Jack, must say, quite an evening. For a minute I had my hands on the Zohar."

"Yes, but I can't say it warded off all harm."

"Please. Let's try again! Please! Please!"

Who could say no to such a plea? But the more immediate problem wasn't the Zohar, not the giant, not the incarceration. It was the toll magnesia water was taking on our digestive tracks. A county jail with little privacy isn't the ideal setting for belly distress. So extreme were our ordeals of evacuation throughout the night that we would readily have traded them in for more bronchospasms.

— *Chapter Nine* —

BALLROOM DANCING

Tabby: "Tabby and Harris here for your Tuesday morning Cap'n Crunch. Lots to report on the latest caper involving the Cardiff Giant. Released from the Schoharie County jail this morning and taken on stretchers to the Bassett Hospital in Cooperstown were Jack Thrasher, investigative reporter for the Discovery Channel, and Esther Federman, hotshot Manhattan shrink. They were caught red-handed trespassing in an abandoned Sharon Springs resort hotel. Fleeing, they said, from the Cardiff Giant, a claim that law enforcement officials have neither confirmed nor denied. We have on the scene our own investigative reporter, Hortense Drew. Hortense, what's the latest?"

Hortense: "As you see behind me, Tabby, police have cordoned off the Hadassah Arms and are sifting clues that the Cardiff Giant may really have been a squatter here. From her sick bed at Bassett Hospital this morning, Dr. Federman claimed that, upon approach of the giant, they dropped a used library book called the *Zoloft* at the entrance to the hotel's synagogue. No *Zoloft* recovered so far. Dr. Federman and Mr. Thrasher have pleaded guilty to a class F misdemeanor and say they seek closure and want to get on with the rest of their lives. Fine, but where might this lead? Doctors at the hospital say the two convicts are suffering from gastritis, bronchial distress, and fleabites, and Dr. Federman has a rampant fungal infection. She and Thrasher declined to discuss how they could come down with so many ailments in so brief a time. They have denied rumors of a romantic liaison, denials many are questioning today. This is Hortense Drew reporting from Sharon Springs. Boy, it stinks here."

Harris: "Thank you *so much*, Hortense! And now let's look ahead to the weekend social calendar. Arriving for your Friday afternoon tea and crumpets in advance of the induction ceremony into the Baseball Hall of Fame will be famed slugger Tony 'the Bat' Homero. The Hotel Otesaga is staging an evening of ballroom dancing in his honor. Most tickets are still available, so ignore the scalpers. As you know, Homero holds the world record for granting interviews to the press despite court orders. Rumor has it his nickname is only in part owing to his skill at baseball. Just kidding, of course. He is also said to be skilled at tango. Who would have thought?"

I listened to this twaddle from my bed at Bassett Hospital, hooked as I was to an IV. Esther was in the adjoining room—an improvement over adjoining jail cells. A night in jail of mutual puking and crapping had done little to strengthen the romantic bond between us—a bond that was already pretty feeble. It didn't take deep insight into the human heart to sense that Esther was not in love with me. Nor I with her. Eros was on the run, if he had ever been nearby. In her eyes I could never be more than a *goyishe kopf*, a goyish blockhead. And as I've hinted, there was a check on my own passion—the emergent feeling I had for Sheila.

Eros apart, I couldn't help but be anxious about Esther's future. Her knack for misdiagnosis seemed even greater than what I'd come to expect of mental health professionals. And her pre-August desertion of clients was risky. Already there were rumblings of a class action suit by these clients, two of whom were now in Manhattan hospitals undergoing electroconvulsive therapy.

That Friday, Tony Homero was chauffeured to the Otesaga in a Lincoln Town Car followed by a Cadillac Seville, a Mercedes S-Class, and a Buick LeSabre, all full of his entourage and bodyguards. Since retiring from the game he had gone into the scaffolding business.

Homero Scaffolds Inc. had a fame of its own, specializing, by all accounts, in early collapse. The catcher defended his company's record, satisfying most observers that the collapses were acts of God to which Homero Scaffolds piously consented.

You see, Homero, a devout Roman Catholic, grew up on Carmine Street in Little Sicily, Manhattan. Wikipedia has an unflattering entry on him, culled here: Son of second-generation Italian immigrants, first of nine children, he earned his neighborhood stripes by painting over parking meters so locals could park for free. Product of Our Lady of Pompeii's early schooling, he believed in saints' relics, vampires, exorcisms, and baked ziti. Once married, he kept his wife too busy as a baby factory to fret about her husband's many rumored infidelities.

Catcher at one time or another for the White Sox, the St. Louis Cardinals, and the Yankees, Homero was strikingly handsome and slender in his earlier years but developed a paunch that grew with every season. The paunch carried the happy message that you don't need steroids and can even go to seed but remain a famous well-performing athlete. He didn't need to run fast anyway because he would belt the ball right out of the park and had broken Mark McGwire's record for most home runs in a single season, and Josh Gibson's and Hank Aaron's lifetime records. More to the point here, he crossed himself before every swing, converting many to his faith whenever a mighty wallop followed. Though the election was close and rancorous, there was no keeping him out of the Hall of Fame.

Like Joe Namath, he bragged about other conquests, claiming the world record for most bedroom home runs. He bragged about everything—and didn't so much walk as swagger. Italian-American families are usually close and mutually supportive, but Homero's many children protested that he must be somebody else's father.

Homero was the subject of caricatures in sports sections of the press throughout the nation. The American Italian Anti-Defamation League routinely objected to these caricatures, both verbal and pictorial, bringing libel suits against esteemed sportswriters and cartoonists. The league lost all these suits because the sportswriters and cartoonists handily demonstrated that their caricatures were literally the case, with no stereotypical cultural enhancements needed. He was, they agreed, hardly representative of Italian-American culture. But what sealed their case was that they had always highlighted his skill at tango.

It was leaked that the league had futilely done a behind-the-scenes intervention, telling Homero to stop being such an easy target for skeptics. Could he at least stop claiming that Mary, mother of God, was behind every wallop?

Ohnstad and his own entourage came through the front door to greet the baseball legend. He spoke through a mike at the podium. Unlike Esther, I had been released from the hospital on Wednesday and joined other press at the hotel's portico. Schoharie County didn't relish our return to their jail cells, so had dropped all charges.

"Mr. Homero, may I be the first to welcome you to Cooperstown, home of the Baseball Hall of Fame, Natty Bumppo, the Ommegang Brewery, the Fenimore House Museum, the Glimmerglass Opera, the life mask of Thomas Jefferson, and, uh, formerly the Cardiff Giant. That's just for starters. Don't worry, no quiz. Mr. Homero has agreed to take some questions from the press." Ohnstad looked ill at ease, clumsily handing the mike to Homero.

"I'd like express my gratitude to Ohnstad here and the folks of Cooperstown for welcoming us like family. And to Mary, mother of God, she's the real mover and shaker behind my getting into the Hall of Fame. I owe it all to Mary, mother of God—and to my own mother, may she rest in peace. You got questions?"

"Tony, what do you make of the recent resignations from the Baseball Writers' Association in response to your admission into the Hall of Fame?" asked the reporter for the *Freeman's Journal*.

Aside to Ohnstad, "*Fatti gatti due, stunod*," Italian-American for "Mind your own business, jerk." Then to the reporter, "They wanna spend more time with their families, capeesh?"

"Tony, what role did your company play in the recent scaffold collapse in Chinatown?" asked the reporter for the *New Berlin Gazette*.

"Basta!" Homero was otherwise tongue-tied. Aside to Ohnstad, "Don't have time for this. Where's the men's room?"

Ohnstad nervously called off the press conference, citing an imminent interview in Homero's suite with a rep from *Dance Magazine*. Homero and company checked into the Otesaga, occupying most of the second floor's east wing, close to my own room.

That Friday evening, the Otesaga's high-ceilinged main dining room, in elegant Georgian Revival décor, was the scene of the Baseball Hall of Fame's first gala of the season. All principals of my small cast were there: Thor Ohnstad, Barry Tarbox, Hazel Bouche, Tony Homero, Tabby Thomas, Harris Scalia, Sheila Drake, Esther Federman—just released from the hospital—and I. Ohnstad had us all seated together and made introductions. The occasion was black tie, and the women were dressed for tango.

"And finally, Mr. Homero," said Ohnstad, "allow me to introduce you to Sheila Drake, set designer for the Glimmerglass Opera."

"Opera? I was just saying to Miss Bouche, I know all about opera. My mother sang the great Puccini arias washing the dishes—"

"Mr. Homero," said Hazel Bouche, not letting Sheila utter a word, "it's not Sheila what's-her-name's business to know anything about opera. I *am* opera and have sung the arias your mother sang and more—in all the great houses of Europe, whenever my horoscope permitted."

"Miss Bouche, I've hit home runs in all the baseball stadiums of the U.S. of A., with Mary, mother of God, looking on, *grazia*."

These two deserve one another, I thought, *and maybe here's a scandal in the making that would appeal to my producers*. So I was a bit put out as the evening progressed that Ohnstad was encouraging Homero to address his fatuities more to Sheila than to Hazel Bouche. And I found it disquieting that Sheila seemed to be warming to Homero. The baseball great's reputation as stud went before him— and it's well known that erotic sensors go deeper than cultural differences. Even a celibate New Age hippy can be drawn to a celebrity buffoon, yes?

In a word, as the evening wore on, I found myself getting jealous. We finished off the banquet fare, most of which was consumed by Bouche and Homero. Bouche gobbled up the crudités and caviar from the lazy Susan before the rest of us got a chance. Homero ate five borrowed drumsticks, and Bouche asked if she could borrow my cherries jubilee, then Sheila's, then Ohnstad's. Well, it's a truism that divas require extra stuffing.

It was time to tango.

When freshly divorced, I took Argentine tango lessons at a dance parlor in Des Moines, learning 5 or 6 of the 160 canonical steps. I was eager at last to put my investment to good use. A little apprehensive of Esther, I played my hand.

"Sheila, let's hit the dance floor."

Esther frowned. She wasn't having a good time anyway, scratching at fungal itch under the table.

Ohnstad intervened. "Sorry, Jack, Tony is guest of honor. He's already asked Sheila for the first dance, right, Tony?"

Homero looked puzzled but was quick on the draw. "Yeah. Sheila, let's tango."

"How did you learn tango, Tony?" asked Sheila. "You're an Italian baseball player, right? As a rule I dislike male athletes."

"Began in the crypt of Our Lady of Pompeii during the Carmine Street *festa*. Parishioners were doing the tango Italian style and priests were shooting craps. Bada bing! This was before I played stickball and Johnny-on-the-pony. My Aunt Matilda—may God rest her soul—she gave me a gift certificate to Arthur Murray's. I was only thirteen but they taught me to tango like Rudolph Valentino, and when my certificate ran out I stole a set of footprint diagrams. Set them out on the Bedford Street sidewalk and charged girls a dime a lesson. Fantastico!"

Sheila looked impressed. "So did you transfer motor skills from tango to baseball?"

"You're a fancy talker, Sheila. *Andiamo a ballare!*"

For her part, Sheila learned the tango during the faded era of her promiscuities, drawn to it because dancers were encouraged to think of themselves as great jungle cats stretching and pouncing. Though she hadn't done it in years, the tango lurked in her muscles. It was paunch-bellied Homero, not I, who was about to tap this muscle memory, stirring up a dormant passional inner life while I warmed the bench.

The floor was cleared for the first couple, just as in the old movies. We all applauded as they strutted center stage and an anachronistic big-sound orchestra, Neal Flotsam and the Jammers, began a medley of tango classics.

Homero crossed himself and led, his cummerbund somewhat confining the midriff bulge, while Sheila's muscular catlike thighs flexed through the slits of her skirt. Her décolleté red silk blouse, straight out of Glimmerglass's costume storage and faintly redolent of mothballs, set off cleavage and collarbones to stunning effect.

As he lifted his head in stylized hauteur, Homero's double chin was minimalized. I watched his thick fingers press Sheila's spine beneath her shoulder blades as their cheeks met and, with arms extended, they did *la salida*, "the beginning," and moved to *el paseo*, "the stroll." Since the tango is a "walking" dance, Homero's inability to run was no handicap, and I could see how the lout routinely finessed his way to first base in matters of the flesh. Leading her slowly through these steps, he injected various *adornos*, "adornments," including *golpes*, "toe taps"—to which Sheila responded with *golpecitos*, "little toe taps."

But these maneuvers were nothing compared to what followed. Zigzags, including *el ocho*, "the figure eight," were followed by *caricias*, "caresses." During a pause, Homero pushed his right leg between Sheila's legs, an *entrada*, and wrapped it around her left knee, then slid his calf down hers. From fifty feet, I thought I could see a shudder ripple up her body. Weren't those goose bumps raising the fine blonde hair on her arms?

Homero was still leading, but Sheila began to turn tables in this tournament of lust. With remarkable bravura and control, she lifted her left leg above her own waist, then allowed her steely calf, now bare, to descend, caressing the back of his right leg.

Sheila led Homero to do *el molinete*, "the wheel," but she usurped the traditional male position at the center. Homero became merely the rim as they spun and spun like binary stars, accelerating and spewing out more and more contagious erotic energy. Homero was now the helpless victim of her will, his face a register of baffled surrender. Proud but pliant only minutes earlier, Sheila was now a ruthless dominatrix.

I averted my eyes in envy and inadequacy, sickened at how this struggle of wills might continue in kind off the dance floor. I watched the others watching. Esther seemed surprised at her half-sister's sudden reversion to bad-bad girl. Ohnstad seemed less surprised than inquisitive, with a raised left eyebrow, wrinkled forehead, and bemused smile.

Chaffing and huffing, Hazel Bouche was eager to show Sheila a thing or two. Renowned for her Carmen, she could dance a raunchy toreador variation on the tango. Tabby and Harris were slyly elbowing one another at a scandal in the making. And finally there was Tarbox looking like a hog in a tux. He gave the dancers a gaping stare such as hedonistic tourists occasion in toothless peasants whenever they drive their rentals through northern German burghs.

Sheila and Homero brought their tango to a close with a *milonga*, best described as a tango in triple time. They finished with Sheila crouched over him like a preying mantis. I joined in the applause, hiding my real feelings. The finale had so winded Homero that he wheezed and collapsed like one of his own scaffolds, but he responded well to oxygen and was soon ready for another number.

All who knew the steps entered the dance floor. I tangoed with Sheila, who had spent her better energies in the duel with Homero. I felt low down on her dance card. And whenever we were near Esther and Thor, who were doing *la cruzada*, "the cross," Esther gave me a painful "back step" in the seat of the pants. Thor seemed unaware of the injury his partner was inflicting, and I was too much the pacifist to retaliate. Partnered by Homero, Hazel Bouche stalked about like Carmen as if to oust all memory of her predecessor. Homero didn't

have much spunk left, but Tabby and Harris overheard him assuring Bouche that he was a true matador in bed.

This left only poor Tarbox without a partner. Just as he placed personals in the local *Pennysaver*, always ending with "must know how to can," so he made the rounds of all the wallflowers, advertising his prowess on the dance floor and asking if anybody had what it takes. Sally Grubb, local manicurist, volunteered, and the two made their way to the center of the busy dance floor. Tarbox walked like a walrus, not even attempting to dodge the dancers' kicks. As it turned out, neither Tarbox nor Sally Grubb could tango. Instead they began jitterbugging with much gusto and little observance of the beat. Flaps of corrugated red skin jiggled over Tarbox's starched rental shirt, as he threw Sally in all directions. It was chaos taking over at the center of measured motion.

One of these thrusts outward hit Thor and Esther, knocking them against Sheila and me, thudding us up against Tabby and Harris, whacking them against Bouche and Homero, who walloped many others in what became a choreography of dominoes. When I picked myself up, I beheld a panorama of fallen tango dancers, bewildered and prostrate before an orchestra that continued to bleat out its tribute to Evita Perón as if nothing had happened.

— *Chapter Ten* —

PLANT SPIRITS

Sheila and I stared at Indian artifacts in the Fenimore House Museum.

"Those are the moccasins I copied for Hazel Bouche," she said. "Huron. My people."

I was doing all I could to win Sheila's favor, and I took appreciative inventory of the black-dyed skin, moose hair, and embroidery.

Our visit to the Thaw Collection of North American Indian Art was a warm-up for our excursion to Gilbert Lake, where Sheila was set on teaching me Plant Spirit Medicine.

I took a chance and alluded to James Fenimore Cooper. "Why did Cooper make a Huron the villain in *Last of the Mohicans*?"

"That's easy. Cooper was of the Devil's party without knowing it. Magua is called a basilisk but he's the real hero—he has all the fire and energy. Remember that scene where he fights Chingachgook hand to hand? Natty Bumppo can't take aim because the two faces keep changing places. You can't tell the villain from the hero."

"So Cooper sits on the sidelines like Bumppo, attracted to his bad Indian and not admitting it?"

"Exactly."

As we viewed an embroidered Huron knife sheath, I tried to tilt this learned conversation toward romance. "Magua's energy is erotic, don't you think? He spends the whole novel pursuing and capturing

Cora, the passionate mulatto. But Cooper bumps them off instead of letting them have their moment. Guess that would make the miscegenation worse, forcing a mulatto to be with an Indian." Note my euphemism—*be with.*

"No, that *is* their consummation," she said spitefully. "Cooper saw that sex is death."

"Oh."

We left the Thaw Collection, went to the Cooper Room, and looked at a Thomas Cole painting based on Cooper's novel. Cora kneels at the feet of the wise Delaware chief, Tamenund, begging for her and her sister's freedom from Magua. Delaware Indians form a large circle around them on a circular plateau. Sublime mountains painted in deep autumnal tones encase the humans.

"You see," said Sheila, "this proves my point."

"How so? Why wouldn't Cora take to Magua? He's energy, she's energy—more than her sister Alice, the good-good girl."

"Cora knows that sex is death—a dark energy that would kill her. She dies anyway, trapped by patriarchy." Sheila grunted the last word.

Before leaving the museum we paid our respects to the macabre exhibit of Browere's life masks of great Americans—squat uncanny busts arranged in yet another oval and conversing grumpily. You have your Thomas Jefferson and John Quincy Adams and Alexander Hamilton. You've got your James Monroe and James Madison and your Henry Clay—and one founding mother, Dolley Madison in her bonnet. Also John Adams, who looked unusually dyspeptic even for his ninety years. Jefferson had almost lost his ears when the plaster hardened too soon and the sculptor was obliged to hammer it off with a mallet. "I now bid adieu forever to busts," he wrote Madison.

"These life masks are nothing to the human-head effigies downstairs, the False Faces," said Sheila, alluding to the spooky wooden masks used by Native American shamans in curing rituals. "Look at Jefferson—that's miscegenation for you. Founding Father as big-time slave owner and rapist of a black woman. White male American heroes are death dealers."

"But Jefferson *was* a gardener, always a young one, he claimed. Maybe he'd be an eager student of Plant Spirit Medicine."

"Too late for him, not for you, Jack."

Though still much attracted to Sheila—and how can I explain such a feeling?—I was finding her a little forbidding. You may have noticed she was really down on men.

The next morning she picked me up in her Jeep Cherokee and we sped at full throttle to Gilbert Lake, a ten-thousand-year-old remnant of glacial melt and excuse enough for a state park. She explained that, like most state parks, you rarely ran into anybody on the trails. Locals either sat next to the small placid lake eating wieners or they holed up in their campers, drinking wine coolers, watching videos, and getting into fights, rarely lethal. It never occurred to anybody to take a hike. Beyond the unused paths and park perimeter were deep forests, as close to wilderness as one could find in the Catskill foothills.

"You know your way around these hills, Sheila?"

"I've been coming here for two years, in training as a Plant Spirit healer. I commune with the plants. Don't laugh."

We parked off Cabin Colony Road and started hiking down Ice Pond Trail. I was wearing my signature Tilley hat. The Canadian company guaranteed it would bring me more adventures.

"Why are you beating on that drum?" I asked.

"Shamanic drumming. It alerts the plants that we're coming as friends. And there's another use—I'll show you shortly. You need to learn patience."

A more immediate consequence of drumming was the scaring of birds and, I hoped, bears. Frankly, I approached this day with more trepidation than a walk in the park normally occasions. As Sheila had explained it, we were about to visit the underworld, the realm of the Plant Spirits. It was scary.

"Why am I carrying this cornmeal?" I was lugging a ten-pound bag of the stuff, organic of course.

"When we approach a plant, we bring an offering. Cornmeal is a favorite of many plants."

"And why the tobacco?"

"Some plants like cornmeal, others prefer tobacco. Don't worry, they'll tell us which they want."

It seemed downright cannibalistic for plants to be eating plants, a scruple I kept to myself. Yes, I was trying to keep virtually everything to myself as I entered Sheila's Plant Spirit Underworld.

Walking past the Ice Pond and heading up a hill toward Spring Pond, beyond which lies the Lake of the Twin Fawns, she talked more about her Huron roots.

"My people were matrilineal—the clan was determined by your mother. And the mothers decided who the clan chiefs would be. My mother was descended from the Turtle clan."

"Didn't the Huron believe the world rests on the back of a giant turtle?"

Her drumming sped up at the question. "Are you making fun of them? There's a deep truth in that belief—deeper than what you've got in male astronomy."

"*Male* astronomy?"

"Look at a telescope. What does it remind you of? Men extending their little penises to distant galaxies. Wishful thinking."

"Never thought of it that way. Well, Galileo did love his daughter."

I needed to watch my mouth. We were getting into delicate territory. Meanwhile, the trail to Spring Pond was becoming more arduous and I was panting under the weight of cornmeal and tobacco.

She was silent for a time, frowning. "The Huron were exploited by the British, the French, the Jesuits, forced to kill beavers for the fur trade. Forced by white men into warfare with the Iroquois. The Beaver Wars and smallpox almost wiped them out."

I couldn't help myself. "Isn't it odd that your mother would marry a furrier?"

"Yes, she should have listened to the Great Spirit. She was sleeping with the enemy. I forgive her. She didn't grasp the difference between our ancestors sacrificing animals out of necessity and white men killing them for profit. Our ancestors always asked the animals for forgiveness. The animals understood and were generous."

"Want to tell me more about your family tree?"

"It's been hard to trace but I know I'm the reincarnation of the eldest daughter of Orontony, the great Huron chieftain."

"How'd you find that out?"

"The Plant Spirit of St. John's wort told me in a dream just last year. This explained everything about me, especially why I was drawn to Plant Spirit Medicine. That's the Huron in me restoring balance and wholeness, trying to make me a whole Huron."

"Just as your half-sister is trying to become a whole Jew?"

"Making fun of us, Jack? Don't. Yes, Esther is seeking her roots too, but real roots aren't Jewish, they're Indian. We're going into the underworld of the Plant Spirits—this means finding our real roots, or at least mine."

We drummed our way by Spring Pond and onto the far side of Lake of the Twin Fawns. As I looked for the fawns, we left the path and headed up into the forest, confronting white ash, black cherry, eastern hemlock, white pines, sugar maples, and at our feet, cinnamon ferns and poison ivy. Chickadees, woodpeckers, chipmunks, red squirrels, and whitetail deer scooted at the beat of our drum.

We hiked a mile or so through bugs and nettles. I was getting nervous. "How do you know which way to go?"

"I've been asking the trees—the maples. Maples are benevolent and wise. They show us the path when there is no path. They're telling us there's a sacred grove of oaks up ahead. That's where we'll speak to the Plant Spirits."

Sure enough, we came across some oaks. I wouldn't have called them a grove, more like a row or scattering. But I kept this to myself, not wishing to prolong our shamanic journey. I was tired and hungry and maybe not so confident that maples have a good sense of direction.

"Okay, Jack. You do the drumming now. We kneel in a prayerful position and get acquainted with these plants." She pointed at a stand of unassuming flowering plants I couldn't identify. "This is mugwort, known for correcting spleen-pancreas imbalance and cooling inflamed cervical vertebrae. Also too much metal in the system." She slowly looked me up and down. "You have too much metal, Jack, and I'm sure you suffer from spleen-pancreas imbalance. How's your back?"

"Right now pretty sore from all the luggage."

"Pulse the drum softly three times a second. We introduce ourselves. Hello, O Spirit of Mugwort, I'm Sheila Orontony and this is Jack Thrasher. We come as friends ... See whether they want cornmeal or tobacco."

I held out a handful of each.

"Shut your eyes and feel which hand is being tugged."

"Hmmm, maybe the right, the cornmeal one."

"Good. Now sprinkle cornmeal all over these plants."

I did so but couldn't see that they were receptive.

"Keep beating. I'm going into a trance and will dream the dream of the Mugwort Plant Spirit. Come along with me."

Her eyes went to the back of her head and she began mumbling something. The Mugwort language, I surmised. Being a good sport, I threw my eyes to the back of my head and began mumbling, all the time pulsing the drum. With a bit of beginner's luck, maybe I too would descend into the Plant Spirit Underworld, playing Paolo to Sheila's Francesca.

After some twenty minutes of this, I was working my way into a trance and seemed to be flying through shadowy air toward Sheila's finely honed haunches, reaching with great erotic hunger when— *splat!*—a grackle let loose its cargo on my forehead. I collapsed backward, awakening Sheila from her trance. She spoke with warmth as I removed my Tilley and wiped off with an oak leaf.

"Jack, the Mugwort Plant Spirit has received our gift and wishes to reciprocate by generous donation of its leaves and flowers." She plucked many of these, asking for forgiveness, readily granted. "Now get the brandy."

Yes, I'd also been lugging a pint of organic brandy in a Mason jar. Into this, she crumbled the leaves and flowers. "This will yield the healing essence of the Mugwort Plant Spirit. It has all the power of acupuncture without the needles. While we wait for it to infuse, I'll do more intake."

Over the past few days she'd asked questions about my medical and psychiatric history, getting into some personal areas such as how often I moved my bowels, how I felt at funerals, whether I would paint my kitchen yellow, what made me throw up, when I wore red pants, and where my sewer water went.

"Now Jack, I'm going to measure your spleen-pancreas imbalance. Give me the incense."

This she lit by rubbing pieces of flint together. She instructed me to hold out my hands and monitored my pain threshold as she touched the burning tip slowly to each of my fingernails.

"Ouch! Ouch! Ouch! Ouch! Ouch! Ouch! Ouch! Ouch! Ouch! Ouch!"

"Yes, everything's out of alignment, not just your spleen-pancreas. Your energy flow is blocked at all the meridians and you are suffering from fire imbalance. Mugwort is the remedy of choice. It's ready now."

She poured some of the brackish liquid into wooden cups. It faintly resembled the sulfuric abomination Esther had inflicted on me, but I gulped it down. "Cheers!"

I'll omit the thanking ritual Sheila performed in the sacred grove. We lunched on tofu, bean sprouts, and organic apricots. It was time to head back. She looked at me with alarm.

"Jack, you're covered with hives!"

"Sheila, you're covered with hives! What's going on?"

Then the hiccups. No ordinary hiccups but huge diaphragmatic upheavals. Assume hives and hiccups through all of what followed.

"The Mugwort Plant Spirit is bringing all our bad Karma to the surface. This is a purging of spirit as energy is transferred from our pancreas to our pineal gland."

I tried to take heart at this. At least hiccups were useful—they took the place of shamanic drumming in scaring off wildlife. We hiked through poison ivy, oak, and sumac—Sheila assuring me through hiccups that the Mugwort Plant Spirit was protecting us from all poisonous plants. Dusk was falling and it seemed to me that we should have come across the path by now. Sheila paused from time to time to ask directions from the maples. Maybe the hiccups made her questions hard for the maples to interpret, because she finally admitted, "We're lost!"

"I've got a cell phone. Let's call for help."

"Cell phone? Not on your life. They cause cancer and they disrupt all the energy lines in our chi."

"Just this once?"

"Absolutely not. Don't even *say* cell phone. We're going to make a lean-to and spend the night. This is fortunate, Jack. Don't you see? The Mugwort Plant Spirit is inviting me to become more of a Huron. We'll be doing nothing more than Indians did before the white man raped the land."

I thought worse things could happen than to bed down with this Huron, so I helped gather branches for our makeshift lean-to.

According to recent surveys, three percent of Otsego County mosquitoes carried the West Nile virus. As we lay down on a poncho, their irritating buzz kept us awake. It would prove difficult to monitor bites because they were indistinguishable from hives.

"More Plant Spirit brandy?"

"Thanks," I said, figuring that a few more hives and hiccups were a small price for getting high. Maybe she would prove seducible.

"You and Homero certainly hit it off on the dance floor last week."

"Oh, Tony—yes, he's been asking me out." These words activated poles of jealousy and envy.

"Oh, well, have you?"

"None of your business, Jack. Do I ask you about Esther?"

"No, but you could."

"Well, I'm not interested."

"But I am—interested in asking *you*."

Solely to avoid death by exposure, she agreed to huddle together in the spoon position on the soggy ground. I wondered if Homero had already felt the taut buttocks against his paunch. Despite the cold and fear of the dark, I felt the itch of arousal. Sheila either didn't mind or didn't notice as we hiccupped through the night.

"I'll say one thing for Homero," I ventured. "He's good at what he does."

"*Very* good!"

I was left to ponder this. I felt jealousy, curiosity, and desire all compounded, but these gave way to alarm when a screech owl screeched. Then about five in the morning I was spooked by the steady thud of approaching footsteps. "Sheila, do you hear that?" I whispered.

The moon was up by now and we could make out dim forms of tree trunks and branches.

"Must be a bear. One Huron clan was the Bear. It won't harm us—or at least me. It'll smell the Bear in me. We must greet it and ask forgiveness."

She began shamanic drumming while I looked around for a club. The footsteps got nearer—maybe one hundred feet away—when I made out the now familiar grinning visage of the Cardiff Giant! We screamed in unison. From the giant came that fiendish gravelly laugh. He turned and thudded away.

One thing was achieved by this encounter: We were cured of our hiccups.

With daybreak we investigated the footprints, easily size eighteen. We could see a trail of broken branches and trampled underbrush. This was evidence enough. I was now a convert to the Cardiff Giant and at least some dimension of the paranormal on this planet.

The reporter in me wanted to follow the breakage and sneak up on the giant. But I hadn't brought my video camera, and anyway, this might mean death. We went off in the direction of the sun, figuring that at least this must be east, wherever east might take us. When we came to a clearing, Sheila said she would gauge my imbalance again to see if the Mugwort Plant Spirit had reconfigured my meridians. She lit the incense.

"Ouch! Ouch! Ouch! Ouch! Ouch! Ouch! Ouch! Ouch! Ouch! Ouch!"

Unfortunately, the tenth "ouch" was accompanied by an involuntary jerk of my hand, which sent the incense up in the air. It landed amid tall grass and lit a fire.

"Let's take off our pants!" I cried. "Use them to put out the fire." I'd learned this in Boy Scouts. We stripped to our undies and started swatting the fire. It quickly burned a circle of some fifty feet in diameter. *Good, all those Plant Spirits are going up in smoke*—a thought I kept to myself. We ran round the perimeter swatting like crazy.

Just as we were bringing the fire under control, a helicopter arrived from the east. Out jumped Thor Ohnstad, accompanied by a cameraman shooting for *The Morning Show*. Needless to say, Sheila and I were embarrassed to be caught on national television with our pants down. Our legs were covered with hives and mosquito bites. The poison ivy, oak, and sumac wouldn't present for another day.

"We've had a search party out for you guys," said Ohnstad. "We saw smoke from the air. You're in luck. But hope we didn't interrupt some primal ritual." He gestured toward our state of undress and chuckled.

"Not what you think, Thor!" Sheila protested. Of course I wished she and I *had* been so engaged. We put our scorched pants back on and got in the helicopter, where we gave the nation an account of our shamanic journey to the Plant Spirit Underworld and the latest sighting of the Cardiff Giant.

Sheila pronounced the outing a success. As we disembarked, she said, "Jack, I'm on my way to becoming a whole Huron, reclaiming my ancestral identity. We were rescued because the Plant Spirits reminded us of the most primal means of communication."

"What's that?"

"Surely you must know, Jack. The language of my people—smoke signals!"

Chapter Eleven

HOLY RAVIOLI

Back at Bassett Hospital, Sheila and I were diagnosed with mild cases of West Nile virus. Lying in my bed with yet another IV attached, I had time to reflect a bit on these people and the string of calamitous events I'd witnessed so far. I'd already been shaken out of my inveterate lethargy. It hadn't taken all that much—just curiosity, erotic yearning, and a limited suspension of the natural order.

The yearning for Sheila was like the ignition of an energy reserve I hadn't known about. It was one of those first-sight infatuations now spreading heat through my frame whether I wanted it or not. She was a wholly inappropriate object of my lust—a celibate, after all. And we were incompatible up and down the line. How could I pretend much longer to honor her solemn New Age investments? She was always talking about energy, and I sensed she had her own reserve. Something I didn't understand was making her a walking paradox: a worshipper of energy who, with little humor, kept it in check. I wanted to know why.

Esther too was an enigma. How could such an intelligent person buy into so robotic an application of the Kabbalah, a mystical tradition esteemed by many notables, including Harold Bloom. It was one thing for a benighted diva to follow her horoscope to the letter or a redneck to believe in alien abduction. It was another for an enlightened psychoanalyst to live her life—from romance to professional practice—in terms of the tetragrammaton, gematria, and *kellipots*.

Does the human brain have a special compartment for the absurd—one that doesn't interfere with other synapses that are making efficient connections with the real world? These people were paying mightily when the real world of poison ivy, fungus, and amoebic dysentery put a kibosh on harebrained notions. They went on believing. Counter-evidence be damned.

Well, it was difficult to admit but now a portion of my own brain had been set aside for the paranormal—in the reanimation, or whatever it was, of the Cardiff Giant. Since this was perking me up in its own way, I didn't reason much about it. On some level I too wished to believe.

I had a partial explanation for Sheila and Esther—they both felt deprived of a full primal identity—Indian and Jewish—and maybe found supplements in hocus-pocus. And come to think of it, I'd arrived in Cooperstown thinking I too was a fragment of a larger personality. But now I could say "Jack Thrasher, Jack Thrasher, Jack Thrasher" to myself and feel that more was accreting around the name, that at last it was beginning to *mean* something.

The greatest enigma, though, was Thor Ohnstad. Beneath the ready but facile sarcasm lurked something more substantial and maybe more sinister, or so I intuited. He was smart, he was the rationalist, he satirized the weak pates of others. But he himself didn't add up. What was the source of his obnoxious nosiness? Why did he take such an interest in me, Sheila, and Esther? Again, I assumed it was something in his past and I was curious. I owed him much for setting me up with Esther and Sheila, but why had he gone to the trouble? This too was an identity enigma. Who was Thor Ohnstad?

Sheila and I improved rapidly. I by eating lots of institutional chicken soup and she by communing with the hospital poinsettia. I declined to tell her that these out-of-season poinsettia were rubber, hoping that fakes might trigger a placebo effect.

The triple scourge of poison ivy, oak, and sumac proved more resistant to treatment. The dermatology department asked if they could photograph us in the nude for the pathology archives. We had made medical history. I said yes, Sheila said certainly not. We were discharged Friday morning with a six-pack of calamine lotion and told to stay out of the woods.

That evening we dined at the Otesaga with Esther, Tony Homero, and Hazel Bouche. The two celebs continued to occasion gossip, having been seen together at the Horned Dorset, an expensive regional restaurant, and at the annual sheep dog trials, where people beguiled the hours watching sheep dogs chase sheep. These trials induced a stupor not unlike a hypnotic trance. Homero claimed to be the world authority on sheep dogs, having owned one, while Bouche claimed to be the world authority on French regional cuisine, having eaten some. Yes, they were a perfect match.

Still, I had my suspicions and was on edge to monitor Sheila's response to Homero. The holder of baseball records and winner of tango competitions also had theological expertise. Mariolatry had been drilled into him at an early age by Carmelite nuns.

"Do you know how Mary, mother of God, got pregnant?" he asked before we'd had time to adjust our napkins.

"The usual method, of course," said Sheila, for whom New Age didn't include virgin birth. She was laughing as she looked up at him. This gave me pause because she rarely laughed. Already she and Homero were talking about sex, maybe sending signals?

"No, there's a painting at my church that shows how it got done. Semen poured out of God's mouth through a long tube that went up Mary's skirt. That's the Immaculate Conception."

"That's disgusting!" said Esther.

"But no evidence against it," I opined.

The Jew in her protested. "Yes, there is evidence. If Mary died a virgin, how do you account for Jesus's brothers and sisters?"

Homero looked stumped. I graciously intervened. "We all should know the answer. They were only half-siblings—Joseph's kids by another woman before he married Mary."

Homero pounded the table. "Yeah, Jack. You tell 'em, goombah. And anyways Mary didn't die a virgin because she didn't *die*. She got, uh, transumped into heaven, body and soul. She's still up there, hasn't aged a minute."

Raised a Southern Baptist, Bouche chimed in. "Yes, she's in the constellation Virgo. You can see her with the naked eye." I thought she must get chilly up there, and what did she do for air?

Esther was squirming, and it wasn't only her fungus. You can write an entire book on the Kabbalah and never mention Jesus or Mary. It's been said, aptly, that Christianity is to Kabbalah what vinegar is to oil. She changed the subject.

"You guys look a mess," she said to Sheila and me, covered as we were with calamine lotion. "Did you expect anybody to believe why you weren't wearing pants?" Esther spoke in jest, but there was spleen attached. Sheila, jolted, dropped her napkin, and I watched from her left side as Homero, sitting to her right, picked it up and returned it to her lap. I was sure his large left hand brushed her thigh.

"Thanks, Tony. No, Esther, you know I wouldn't butt in on your little thing. Jack's all yours."

Was her use of "butt" another signal to Homero? And "little thing," hmmm. Of course, you know by now that I didn't wish to be all Esther's. I wished to be all Sheila's.

"The Kabbalah teaches that nobody *belongs* to another. Jack's as much yours as he is mine."

Sheila once again dropped her napkin, and I watched Homero again pick it up and slyly brush along her thigh and maybe her belly. I swear I saw her wriggle a bit in response.

Thor Ohnstad passed by our table and recommended the homemade lobster ravioli. He had hired a new chef with great pasta credentials away from a restaurant in Little Italy. There was a surplus of the ravioli because many hotel guests had departed earlier that day, fleeing the West Nile virus.

"Sheila," he chortled, "did you expect anybody to believe why you and Jack weren't wearing pants?"

In response to this witless remark, Sheila yet again dropped her napkin. Ohnstad and Homero both went for it, Homero winning out and again marking territory.

What happened next is for the history books. Well, this *is* a history book. The ravioli arrived and Homero fell over backward in his chair, his head thumping the floor. He picked himself up and announced, "The face of Mel Gibson is in my ravioli!"

We all looked at his plate. Sure enough, one piece of ravioli was notably larger than the others and irregular in shape. There, in semi-profile, was the canonical face of Mel Gibson.

"Praise the Lord," cried Bouche and Homero simultaneously. "It's a miracle!" Other guests in the dining room gathered round to witness the ravioli. "Let's call in the bishop!" declared Homero.

Ohnstad approached and confirmed that it did look like Mel Gibson. "I'll inform Tabby and Harris—this could be good publicity."

Meanwhile, even spiritual people need to eat. Homero ate the adjacent lay ravioli, leaving only the holy ravioli at the center of his plate. "Waiter, bring me some Saran Wrap and a doggie bag. I'm taking this here to the church."

We all piled into his Lincoln Town Car, chauffeur at the ready, for the quick ride to St. Mary's Roman Catholic Church on Elm Street.

Homero strutted down the aisle and got the attention of a young priest conducting evening mass in his running shoes. "Father, behold this ravioli. See, it's the goddam face of Mel Gibson. Declare a miracle."

This the priest promptly did, repeating the declaration to the mass media upon the arrival of Tabby and Harris, attended by their crew. Thus, they—not I—first broadcast the remarkable news. But I was an eyewitness to the event, and this cheered my Discovery Channel producers.

Within hours of the installation of the Holy Ravioli, the faithful began to queue up for a look. Soon the line stretched all the way down Elm Street and around the corner. And as you undoubtedly already know if you have read other histories of the period, this was only the beginning. The church received a congratulatory phone call from the president of the United States, hoping to curry favor with Catholics in time for his reelection. All the major networks and CNN gave it top billing. More than one hundred websites sprouted. After five days an entire town-within-the-town sprang up, taking over the Otsego County Fairgrounds.

Describing this community will tax my powers of narration. John Bunyan's Vanity Fair couldn't hold a candle to this assortment of tents, campers, trailers, SUVs, and painted vans taken off cinderblocks for the occasion. You might call it a microcosm of the whole damned human race in the early twenty-first century, more than two centuries after Voltaire, Gibbon, and Diderot declared an end to miracles. Though predominantly Christian, the population embraced a wealth of collateral beliefs and practices.

Ohnstad and I walked through the fairgrounds one evening, entering the stadium where auto demolition derbies were normally held.

"It's boosted the economy just when we needed it. These people aren't scared of the West Nile virus," he said.

"No, they're immune by grace of God."

Many had come seeking cures. Television networks had crews and reporters lined up at the church exit to get firsthand testimonials. "Look, Pam, my feet aren't flat no longer. Thank you, Mel." "The bursitis is practically gone, dear Lordy." "The hair loss has abated. Praise you, Mel, and you too, Jesus."

The statue of Mary to the left of the central apse began weeping crystal tears.

In the gloaming, Ohnstad and I made our way through the makeshift town, where people already had their miniature yards festooned with rubbish. Like was seeking out like. Over charcoal grills and amid the stench of lighter fluid, groups huddled according to their convictions. In one corner we encountered spiritualists trying to raise a card table. In another, tattooists were offering indelible images of the Blessed Virgin at reduced rates. Satanists were performing a black mass with sluggish copulations on an improvised cardboard altar. Psychics were peering into purple balls while monitoring reality television. An Alien Abduction Focus Group swapped stories and scanned the sky. New Age devotees stood in their underwear and gauged one another's chakras and meridians. There was no water underfoot, so dowsers sought out the Devil's footprints. A rusty trailer became a studio for Kirlian photography where hawkers guaranteed orange auras and a halo to boot. The colonic irrigation folk were on the perimeter, close to the public facilities. Five channelers were competing for Queen Cleopatra—all went into trances and emitted her voice, though how she was able to converse simultaneously on five different frequencies was beyond me. Many others were getting calls from the dead over cell phones. "Hey, Louie, it's for you—your mama. She sounds pissed."

Transcending such focus groups, the universal human practices of spouse swapping, buggery, larceny, fibbing, braggadocio, drunkenness, gluttony, and flatulence were much in evidence.

Perhaps I sound a little moralistic, even elitist. But remember I'm a reporter and give you only the facts as I observe them, without garnish or inflation. And in no way do I mean to scuttle these various enterprises and belief systems—I try to keep an open mind. My touchstone is Hamlet's caveat to Horatio, that there are more things in heaven and earth . . . You know the rest.

Remember, I myself had come to believe in the Cardiff Giant, at least in some measure. If he was one of those "things," surely there were others.

Thor Ohnstad and I were waxing philosophic as we waded through this human fen. "Do you think science and religion are necessarily at odds, Thor?"

"Well, sport, just between us, I take a dim view of religion. Unusual in a businessman, I know. But I'd rather hear an inspirational speaker tout the higher mission of a cutlery company than suffer through a prayer breakfast."

"My hunch is that the paranormal isn't in quite the same bailiwick with religion. You can test paranormal claims. Does ESP work? Is that really your dead mother's voice on the answering machine?"

"Yes, but how do these differ from religious-nut claims?" he asked. "Can't we test whether that rube was cured of flat feet? Just look at his feet! Can't we test whether prayer works? Just see if ten hours of fervent prayer can pop a pimple!" Ohnstad was warming to the topic. "I lump the paranormal and the religious together—it's all superstition. Richard Dawkins agrees with me. That's not to say they're worthless—the human race needs its superstitions to get through the day. Just look at our women!"

"Our women?"

"Yes—I mean *your* women now. Sheila. Esther. Their noodles are full of stuff and nonsense. Why did that happen?"

"Why indeed?"

"Blame some of it on suffering and deprivation at an early age—that furrier father," he said. "But there's more to it than that, we can be sure."

"They give him very bad press."

"Sheila's down on men. Guess she makes some kind of exception for you."

"Not really," I sighed.

He paused, then asked, "Have you noticed she seems to make an exception for Homero too? Unlikely, I know, but there's evidence."

"What do you mean?" I was getting nervous.

"You saw them tango. That buffoon touched a button our girl's kept in hiding for years. Did you see her dropping her napkin at dinner? Maybe doing it on purpose so he'd pick it up?"

"Any evidence they've been seeing each other . . . or sleeping together?" I asked this with fake nonchalance and held my breath.

"Not sure what's going on there. No nasty with Homero for the past few days at least. You were in the woods with her, then the hospital. But earlier I was having trouble getting hold of her—she wasn't picking up. Has that place by herself out in Cherry Valley, you know. And—come to think of it—those were the same times I was having trouble getting hold of Homero. Could be one of those improbable liaisons founded on lust alone. I've always felt Sheila conceals a volcano—no telling who might tap it. Maybe some lucky rube like Homero. You never know."

I listened in loathing and despair. Volcano? That's the same metaphor that had occurred to me. Move over, Othello. At least the Moor made the two-backed beast with Desdemona. I hadn't got to first base with Sheila.

Blame this last metaphor on Homero. The next day would bring his induction into the Hall of Fame. Then, he would have no excuse to stay in Cooperstown.

I prayed for his departure.

— *Chapter Twelve* —

THE INDUCTION

Harris: "Tabby and Harris here for your Sunday morning cornmeal with navy beans and bacon. No recent sightings of the Cardiff Giant, but this is a great day for Cooperstown and the American Dream. Four players will be inducted into the Baseball Hall of Fame, including Tony 'the Bat' Homero, whose baseball fame has been happily overshadowed by his discovery of the Holy Ravioli. I'm honored to emcee the induction. Cooperstown has risen from a one- to a two-fold Mecca. Whether you're a baseball buff or a Mel Gibson afficionado, you'll find the right stuff in our little village."

A record thirty-two thousand people crammed into the Clark Sports Center at 1:30 p.m. for the ceremony. The numbers swelled because many squatters at the county fairground had tired of follow-up audiences with the Holy Ravioli and were looking around for more action. The governor and baseball commissioner were in attendance, sitting on a platform along with thirty-three grizzled veteran Hall of Famers, four corpulent inductees, one Hazel Bouche, one Thor Ohnstad, and one Harris Scalia. I was standing under a hot sun with Sheila and Esther—all of us still scratching at residual hives, fungus, blisters, and mosquito bites.

"The famed mezzo Hazel Bouche will sing the national anthem," announced Harris.

Hazel gave Homero a shameless grin as she paraded across the platform. His wife and ten spawn leaked to the press that, in response to reports of his misbehavior, they were boycotting the ceremony. Hazel Bouche announced that she wouldn't sing for another twenty minutes since only then would the benefics Venus and Jupiter overcome the malefics, Mars and Saturn, indicating the time was propitious for an Aries, whose element is fire, to begin the outthrusting of will into the universe.

The crowd took this explanation well enough, but the delay worsened the sweaty stench. After Bouche belted out the national anthem ear-shatteringly, converting many right away to the zodiac, the governor announced that he wasn't throwing in the towel, that he would continue to fight the latest statewide efforts to recall him for gross malfeasance. The baseball commissioner, who sat on the board of directors of a major chewing-tobacco firm, announced that because of recent resignations from the Baseball Writers' Association, which elects players to the Hall of Fame, he would be submitting a list of replacements. It was rumored that he made all such decisions with a Ouija board.

Then began the speeches of the inductees. No one would have wished them longer. The first was an exercise in thanking, with the player's agent at the top of the list. The next two spoke of American values and how their own careers epitomized all that was best about free agency in the land of the free.

While these speeches wore on, Barry Tarbox and his deputies moved stealthily through the crowd, asking young women whether they or anybody they knew had had sex with the Cardiff Giant.

At last it was time for Homero, who, we hoped, would enliven this leaden ritual. We weren't disappointed. He stood at the podium, adjusted his genitals, and crossed himself. "I owe all this to Mary, mother of God, and to Mel Gibson. I personally discovered Him in the ravioli. Somebody else might have eaten that ravioli, but I'm always on the lookout for Mel Gibson in ravioli, and at the conclusion of this ceremony, you gotta visit the church on Elm Street. Tell the

Lord that Tony 'the Bat' sent you. Got some problems with your digestive track or your liver or your dick? Ask the Lord to heal! Admission's only fifty cents."

A few in the audience, including the baseball commissioner, seemed uneasy at so large a dose of religion in a secular ceremony. Then something truly bizarre happened. As Homero spoke, other voices were heard over the loudspeaker, fading in and out, voicing over and under Homero's own utterance. He looked puzzled but wasn't about to yield the podium to a chorus of unseen speakers. Sheila, Esther, and I strained to make out these other voices. Sometimes they seemed to be speaking Italian, sometimes English, then what sounded like a parakeet speaking German. The words were not quite intelligible.

Then it struck me—we were hearing electronic voice phenomena, first investigated by the Latvian psychologist Konstantin Raudive, whose authoritative book on the subject, *Breakthrough*, was published in 1971. He asked whether these voices breaking through our electronic lines of communication were extraterrestrials, the dead, angels, or satanic spirits. Take your pick.

How do I know this? From a Discovery Channel special, of course. Many in the audience must have seen the same special because a wave of recognition swept through the sports center.

"Hey, Mom, is that you?" asked Homero of one of the doleful Italian voices. "*Che cozz?* Sit tight for a minute, let me get on with my speech."

Sheila said, "It's the Mugwort Plant Spirit telling us not to overrate baseball—a guy sport."

Esther heard the voices differently. "It's the *Malakhim*— messenger angels telling us to obey the 613 commandments."

Others were sure they heard their own voices since they were already having out-of-body experiences and, in some cases, undergoing bilocation, an ingenious procedure that permitted a person to be in two different places at the same time. Other explanations were buzzed about. I overheard talk of alien choirs in space, astral bodies, psychokinesis, channeling, and poltergeists. Tarbox was convinced it was the Cardiff Giant.

But it was the born-again Christians who held greatest sway. As the discoverer of the Holy Ravioli and now God's intermediary, Tony Homero was, for want of better, the Second Coming. Hundreds of the faithful swept toward the podium, thinking a few swatches from his garments might have the true grit of the Shroud of Turin. "Tony! Tony!" Within minutes Homero was stripped bare, pathetically holding his privates while the governor, the commissioner of baseball, and Harris Scalia looked on.

"Where's my plaque?" Homero cried.

The baseball commissioner consulted his Ouija board and made a solemn pronouncement. "For the first time in the history of the Baseball Hall of Fame, an inductee will be *de*ducted simultaneously with his induction. Mr. Homero, for triggering this travesty, I am withholding your plaque. You're out of here!"

— Chapter Thirteen —

LOCKED IN

I got locked into the Baseball Hall of Fame after hours. I'd fallen asleep in the men's room at closing. I was so battered, poisoned, and bitten since arriving in Cooperstown—and pumped so full of antibiotics, emetics, valium, and anti-inflammatories—that I wasn't steady on my feet and was prone to narcosis.

Upon awakening and exiting the men's room, I entered the antechamber to the Hall of Fame gallery, eerily lit only by small exit fixtures. To my left was the life-sized statue of Babe Ruth swinging. I paused and looked again, startled to see his broad squat features change into the grinning pig snout of Barry Tarbox. And that was no baseball bat—rather, an alien restraint net fluttered toward me as I tried to escape into the gallery, my body so heavily weighted I could barely move.

Inside the gallery, I heard Tarbox oinking after me as I struggled down the corridor amid the plaques. Was that Ted Williams at the far end? The statue moved, the belly became distended, and the form of Tony "the Bat" Homero strutted up the ramp toward the Bullpen Theatre.

I have a gentle nature, am a well-behaved Midwesterner, but the sight of Homero filled me with rage. Thinking to tear him apart, I ran in pursuit, passing by Robert Redford peering out from a billboard.

This was all "only natural," he said with cool. *Only natural?* It all seemed to me totally perverse. When I entered the Bullpen Theatre I saw Homero sink into the movie screen where he was featured in a short loop. He was hitting ball after ball out of the stadium, in the jerky manner of a mechanical wooden puppet, to the sound of "Take Me Out to the Ballgame." I would be spending eternity trapped in this loop if I didn't quickly exit—so I ran to the second floor, passing through the gallery, "Pride and Passion."

Yes, the museum was a repository of American culture. Here they were, the Negro Leagues. There I beheld the Birmingham Black Barons walking through the Colored Entrance. There stood Jackie Robinson, ready to break into the majors. And there was Willie Mays running, his glove extended for all eternity to make the greatest catch ever—off the bat of Cleveland's Vic Wertz—and doing his inimitable pirouette. *Good*, I thought, *Black players are getting their due.*

But my eyes widened as Willie Mays metamorphosed into Hazel Bouche. She had baseballs for boobs and announced, "Black is beautiful. I'm not pitching till Neptune has passed out of the second house of Uranus." Universal boos and pandemonium at Ebbets Field.

I feared she would set back Black liberation and feminism many years, so I pleaded. "Miss Bouche, please pitch—don't do this to your brothers and your sisters!"

"Mind your own business, pork chops."

I ran up another flight to the "Women in Baseball" gallery. "All American Girls," read the legend. Here I felt safe for a time and gazed on a blown-up photograph of the Vassar College Resolutes of 1876. The nine women were solemn and resolute. One of them was uncannily familiar. I peered in the dim light and beheld Sheila Drake wearing a ravioli necklace. Her features were now more Native American than Irish. Instead of a mitt she held a papoose. *Whose child is that?* I wondered—and was spooked to see that the features were distinctly Italian-American.

I mustered courage to speak to her, whispering, so that the eight others wouldn't take umbrage. I wanted to declare my passion and to ask an overwhelming question, like *How do you explain yourself to yourself?* My words were all wrong. "You ask why I'm so obsessed with you. Not sure. You're deficient in humor, have to say. Esther takes jokes about Kabbalah rather well—but you're so solemn about those weirdo Plant Spirits. They got us in a lot of trouble. And you hate men, so why the devil are you having sex with Homero? Pardon the psychology, but is it masochistic mutilation or narcissistic self-indulgence? And that's not all. There's something weird going on with you and Ohnstad. And last, not least, your identity thing. Identity! Dammit, why not settle for one-fourth Huron?"

This interrogation seemed more and more banal as I klutzily covered one sentence over with another. I felt my blood pressure rising, my temples pulsing. Sheila looked at me sternly. Then she stepped effortlessly out of the photograph, handing her papoose to the pitcher, and headed toward the "Baseball Cards" gallery. She was buck naked and carried a sprig of daisies. "He loves me, he loves me not," she chanted to the Daisy Plant Spirit. I watched her silently from behind. The spectacle of her jaunty butt, long auburn hair, and poison ivy blisters set off a craving.

I approached the "Baseball Cards" gallery and was disappointed that naked Sheila had morphed into fully clothed Esther. She was taking notes while she read the cards, singling out Hank Greenberg, Mordecai Brown, Marv Rotblatt, Joe Ginsberg, Bud Swartz, Al Rosen, and Micah Franklin. Concerning Mordecai Brown, I heard her exclaim, "Six consecutive seasons of twenty wins or more—six and twenty are sacred numbers! And he had only three fingers on his pitching hand. Three's a sacred number! Jack, hi there. This explains why Mordecai Brown beat Christy Mathewson in nine consecutive games. Nine's a sacred number, divisible by three."

"Esther, you and I have had high adventures together, in and out of bed, but I was rather hoping you were your half-sister. I'm beginning to think I'm dreaming—and I'd like to play out a fuck fantasy with her. Been nursing it for many weeks, you know."

Esther flung a fistful of baseball cards in my face and said, "Jack, your gematria just doesn't add up. Okay, if you must, she went thataway."

I headed toward the "Major League Locker Room," where I saw the statue of a man with huge ears and no sign of Sheila, who shouldn't have been hanging in a men's locker room anyway. The man, Casey Stengel, whirled about and took on the features of Thor Ohnstad.

"I'm manager here," said Ohnstad. "Are you looking for Sheila? I just saw her. She was looking for Homero, sweating big time."

Ohnstad smirked. There was something about this man I did not like. His manner of interrogation, his Rotarian heartiness on top of sarcasm, his innuendoes about Sheila and Homero. This was a locker room and I feared he might take down his pants, so I kneed him in the nuts and ran to the staircase where the world's largest baseball bat is mounted—eleven feet long and of considerable girth, circa 1936.

What I saw beneath it filled me with equal measures of dread and desire. Naked except for some wampum she wore about her neck, Sheila had mounted Homero and was taking her pleasure to tango music. I approached from behind and witnessed the intensity of her ride. Flanking them were Tabby and Harris holding cameras for reality television. Homero and Sheila caught sight of me and increased their tempo.

"Holy ravioli, how I like the way you move," said Homero. "Keep it up, *bellissima*."

Sheila kept it up, looking at me sympathetically. "Don't worry, Jack. I can take him or leave him. This is meaningless. It's not half as sexy as it looks."

Reassured, I looked down at Homero but saw that he was now the Cardiff Giant. He smiled and spoke the first real words yet attributed to the giant, who must have been no mute golem after all. "Jack, maybe after I've finished you'd like to take a turn at the throttle?"

"Nothing doing!" I cried, as I whacked him with the 1936 bat and awakened wide-eyed to the exhortations of the morning janitor.

— *Part Three* —

TO THE OTHER SIDE

— *Chapter Fourteen* —

THE BENEFIT

Harris: "Tabby and Harris here again for your Sunday morning prune Danish. As you may have heard, there have just been three well-intended but botched assassinations in South America, a feminist coup in Iran, an earthquake in Florida, and the announcement by SETI that contact has been made with folks living on a planet in the Big Dipper. But let's turn straightaway to what really concerns us: the lives of the celebs and the social calendar."

Tabby: "Last night's closing of the Glimmerglass Opera season was marred by cabbage hurled at the renowned diva, Hazel Bouche. Not to editorialize, but we find this in poor taste. Miss Bouche was within her rights to break off an aria in *Don Carlo* to explain that with Mercury the messenger now retrograde in Virgo and the New Moon recently in her solar sixth house, and because of the close association of aria with Aries, and considering the only colors for an Aries yesterday were grape and pale lilac—the costumer had proved clueless—it was for the good of the production that she cease projecting her elemental fire into the universe."

Harris: "She asked her current boy toy, Tony 'the Bat' Homero, to take a bow. The audience threw more cabbage. But why, forevermore? Homero has, as you know, lingered in Cooperstown begging the baseball commissioner for a pardon after the Hall of Fame debacle. He sits daily at the stoop of the hall, pouting and asking '*che cozz?*' of his bodyguards. Not to editorialize, but we hope the commissioner lets the poor putz into the Hall of Fame so he'll clear out of town."

Tabby: "This evening, the elite of Cooperstown will attend the annual benefit for the restoration of Hyde Hall. It's being thrown, as usual, by the local benefactor Thor Ohnstad at the Busch Mansion. Ohnstad has just announced his candidacy for governor in the recall election."

Tabby and Harris together: "Not to editorialize, but let's hope he loses, for the good of the union."

I accompanied Esther and Sheila to the benefit in Esther's rental Mercedes. As usual, Ohnstad was right: The Busch Mansion was a mishmash of Colonial Revival and Queen Anne & Shingle, also a touch of American Arts & Crafts. Turrets, cupolas, dormers, deep striped awnings, oriel windows, a wraparound porch, and a terraced front lawn—all befitting this Midwestern parvenu and Gatsby redux. How dare Ohnstad call me "sport"? He hadn't even read *The Great Gatsby*. Yes, this mansion embodied Ohnstad himself, a quirky fellow full of contradiction, a human pastiche.

In the spacious lawn and garden, gazeboes were scattered about, set off by antique statuary—nymphs, satyrs, and peeing cherubs. Here we beheld the top crust of Cooperstown. But Ohnstad had made some egalitarian gestures. Riffraff with no intention of donating to Hyde Hall could scarf down hors d'oeuvres. I spied a support group of ageing county-fair beauty queens binging on the pimento-and-horseradish cheese dip.

Sheila, Esther, and I had just begun tossing off New York State Goat White when up walked an unprepossessing man. Short, balding, with thick glasses, in his early forties, wearing a yarmulke and string tie, and carrying a fiddle, he pointed quizzically to Esther and me. "I've seen the two of you somewhere before . . ."

"The opera?" she suggested.

"No, no . . ." He paused, squinted, and exclaimed, "Yes, Sharon Springs! You were the ones I observed breaking into the Hadassah

Arms. When you were arrested, I was stationed in the backseat of the other police car."

"Thanks a lot," I said.

"We owe lots to you," hissed Esther. "Like a night in jail."

"Please do not take it personally. I did my duty. You had a mission, Dr. Federman, and used extreme means. I too am a Jew. I was on duty as neighborhood sentinel that evening. I too have a mission. I am financing the restoration of Sharon Springs. Mr. Ohnstad hopes I shall have funds leftover for Hyde Hall."

"Don't give him a shekel," said Esther, quickly impressed. "Save it for Sharon Springs. How'd you get interested?"

"My grandparents used to take the waters there."

"So did mine. What's your name?"

"Deronda. Daniel Deronda."

"Hmmm, I know that from somewhere. Didn't we see it in the Zohar, Jack?"

"I do not subscribe to Kabbalah, practicing mainstream cultural Judaism, but my grandparents did. They used to speak of the 'minor metaphysics of the smile.' I remain unclear as to what was meant by it."

"I can tell you!" said Esther, warming to the very man who had given her a criminal record. "It's a kabbalistic version of yin and yang. In the Talmud it is written that 'the searching taste of your eyes is better than wine, and the smile of your teeth is better than milk.'" She smiled at Deronda with her teeth. "Rabbi Yohanan explained the passage—it means the whiteness of teeth offered to a friend is better than a nice glass of milk."

"Ah," said Deronda. "Thank you for the information."

I knew when Esther was flirting. Deronda did not. He paused. "I have always thought it my duty to stay with the traditional teachings."

Undeterred, Esther began an interrogation of dutiful Deronda rivaling Ohnstad in nosiness. Such is the prerogative of an analyst. Pretty soon Sheila and I, into our third glass of Goat White and looking on, knew more about this stranger than we knew about each other.

I'll summarize: His surname derived from *Ronda*, the Spanish town from which the Sephardic Jews were evicted in 1492, some of them heading east to the Ottoman Empire. Daniel Deronda's paternal grandfather emigrated from Salonika in 1910 and set up a ladies handbag shop on Orchard Street in the Lower East Side. With an immigrant's industry and a willingness to cooperate with goyim, he prospered, married his accountant, and, twenty visits to Sharon Springs and sixty thousand handbags later, passed out of this existence, leaving his eldest son enough seed money to embark on a rapacious career in Manhattan real estate. The son's methods included buying up buildings inhabited by Polish and Ukrainian widows in the East Village and Lower East Side, waiting for them to die when he wasn't able to evict, then raising the rent. Bonding with his grandfather, Deronda was now making amends for the sins of his deceased father, putting the ill-gained family wealth into good works and restoring the community that offered his grandparents their only respite from a life of honest toil, thrift, and calculation.

Esther clearly liked what she was hearing. They shared Sharon Springs and loathsome fathers, and they bonded with a grandfather. "This is fascinating! But you must tell me more about your mother."

Deronda looked down at his feet and sighed as if he would prefer not to. "My mother is, how shall I say it, a Jewish mother. She recently sent me a pair of earmuffs from Emile's Thrift Shop. Yes, earmuffs. I know it is summer. And she sends ample advice."

"About women and how to avoid them?" asked Esther, laughing.

"Frankly, yes. I moved out of our apartment only last year to test the waters on my own. You see, I too am a caricature. For example, if I arrange a social visit, I must include my mother. She helps out with the conversation." Deronda again looked down at his feet. "You see, Dr. Federman, my rabbi runs an online dating service. But it is not what you think."

"How do I sign up?" asked Esther.

"You cannot if you are not already a member of our synagogue," he said with emphasis. "You would not be given the password."

Deronda didn't seem to be taking the bait, so Esther tried a tactic that would have unforeseeable consequences. Philosophers call this sort of thing *moral luck* or, better, moral *bad* luck.

Turning to me, she said, "Jack, you for one are not a member of my synagogue. How could *we* ever manage?"

She tritely pinched my right cheek, trying to ignite Deronda by flirting with another man. Darwinians call this *mating display*, I call it child psychology.

Hoping that Esther would indeed find a man more suitable than I, I played along. "Where there's a will, there's a way. Look, I'll leave the Muggletonians, convert and join your synagogue, and get the password from your rabbi."

"Keep it up," whispered Esther.

Assume a quarter hour of inane dialogue between Esther and me, while Sheila sullenly guzzled Goat White and Deronda uneasily looked on. I paid Esther compliment after compliment, mercifully omitted here. But the effect was less to stoke Deronda's fire than to stir up Sheila's yellow bile. I was tapping a vein I had not fully registered before.

"Mr. Deronda, a word to the wise. You won't score with my sister if your gematria doesn't add up." She swilled more Goat White, a wine so sweet that it induces a kind of diabetic high.

"Hmmm," Esther calculated, obviously interested in the question. "The name *Daniel* is forty-six, I think."

"Forty-six. That number must be either perfect or sacred," I said hopefully.

Esther was silent. Clearly this number was nowhere. And I feared Deronda was staying in the wrong room.

Sheila turned her animus toward me. Strange that a Plant Spirit healer would even have animus.

"You're big with the compliments this evening, Mr. Jack Thrasher." She kicked my right shin. "Maybe Es hasn't told you some other things about herself, like her bulimia and kleptomania and the chronic papillomavirus."

"Her what?" asked Deronda.

"Sheila, hush! Don't believe a word of this, Mr. Deronda." Esther took a gulp of Goat White and retaliated. "Jack, has Sheila told you about her affair with Thor?"

"Esther, shush! Okay, you asked for it. Jack, has my sister told you about *her* affair with Thor?"

I silently questioned whether Plato was right when he declared wine to be the greatest gift of the gods. Sheila's affair with Thor? I had intuited this long ago but didn't know what to make of it. And Esther's affair with Thor? I had taken him at his word—it was short-lived.

"That's a fib!" replied Esther. "You know damned well that Ohnstad and I never . . ." She looked at Deronda, who was shifting from one foot to another as if getting ready to shuffle off. "You know the expression, Mr. Deronda, this goy and I never 'prepared the mattress of love.'"

"Thank you for the information."

"You narcissistic twit," said Esther to Sheila. "It's your father's fault that my mother is in her grave."

"It's *your* father's fault that I was sexually abused."

"But I was just now under the impression," ventured Deronda, "that you two young ladies *shared* a father—a furrier father, if I am not mistaken."

This was the first I'd heard of sexual abuse. I feared the exchange was about to end in sororal mud wrestling when Ohnstad rang the cowbell. He stood next to a large statue of Silenus, took the mike, and began uttering benefit platitudes. I tuned him out and scanned the gathering. Tabby and Harris's crew had cameras and mikes everywhere, picking up stray and damning remarks. There was overlap with the Glimmerglass crowd of facelifts and drool. Some of the Holy Ravioli crowd had crashed the party, thinking another revelation might be at hand, maybe this time in the German sausage. And I noticed that the county-fair queens were peering in our direction.

Sheila and Esther breathed heavily and seethed on both sides of me. I try hard not to be a male chauvinist but couldn't help puzzling over all the fashionable talk of a sisterhood. I felt caught 'twixt mighty opposites and prayed Ohnstad's speech would last long enough for bile to subside. Having acknowledged the top donors of the Friends of Hyde Hall and called for increased donations, he passed along to other matters.

"As you know, Cooperstown has recently been the scene of eerie happenings. I need not remind you of the disappearance of the Cardiff Giant. Jack Thrasher and Sheila Drake have had the most recent sighting. The giant is for real, and Sheriff Tarbox is judicious in concluding there may well be aliens in our midst."

Guests looked apprehensively to their left and right, while I pondered the hypocrisy of this seasoned skeptic adding to the paranormal craze. Granted, I was now a reluctant believer in the giant, but Ohnstad had no right to be, whatever the gain in local revenues.

"I personally thank Tabby and Harris for spreading the word. But I must fault the current governor for not following the counsel of his own I Ching oracle. He should order the National Guard up here to protect the citizenry. When I'm governor I'll see to it that the giant is caught and the aliens get sent packing. And that the Holy Ravioli gets irradiated. Say, folks, has anybody seen the great Homero?"

I was looking around for Homero and had taken note that Hazel Bouche, never far from the smorgasbord, was unaccompanied. Would Sheila be leaving shortly for a rendezvous with "the Bat"?

"And now may I lean on your generosity and urge that, beyond the coffers of Hyde Hall, you make a contribution to the Ohnstad-for-governor campaign chest!"

Anemic applause followed this indiscreet appeal. I was embarrassed for Ohnstad. But he continued with a surprise announcement. "Friends of Hyde Hall and other guests, I now have the honor of introducing Danny Deronda, famed master of klezmer bluegrass, who will entertain us with a medley of Catskill Mountain melodies. Danny, take the mike!"

"My God!" exclaimed Esther. "That's how I know your name. *Danny* Deronda. You are hot!"

"It is only my avocation," said Deronda, who walked stiffly to the mike and without smiling stuck his fiddle under his chin, which I now saw had a prominent fiddler's callus. He blinked a few times while registering the crowd through thick specs—most were still guzzling, chomping, and chattering—and, without saying a word, began to fiddle.

Within seconds this prodigious talent had silenced even the ageing beauty queens. All at once transformed from stiff stick to pliant river reed, he entered into a trance not unlike Yo Yo Ma at the cello, lunging forward and tilting back dramatically, making the instrument laugh and cry by turns. Such bluegrass standards as "Foggy Mountain Breakdown," "Truck Driving Man," and "Dill Pickle Rag" reappeared as Jewish klezmer. He was making American mountain music fuse with the spirit and intonation of shtetels and urban ghettos, the double stops and hot licks of bluegrass augmented by the weeping ornaments and trills of the Eastern European fiddle. Entranced along with the rest of us, Esther became a Danny Deronda groupie on the spot.

When he shifted gears and began playing a Yiddish Bulgar, or circle dance, the ageing county-fair beauty queens mistook it for a square dance and began to do-se-do. Squares don't mix well with circles, so this unseemly misappropriation made Deronda snap out of his trance. He stopped playing after only two Bulgars and reconverted to a stiff stick while people applauded warmly. He bowed formally, said "Thank you kindly for your attention," and rejoined us. Esther gaped at him as if he were Moses de Léon. Though all of us had been floored by his exquisite, impassioned music, Deronda himself now looked as if nothing had happened.

Ohnstad announced that Deronda CDs could be purchased near the cherubs, and the benefit began to peter out. Sheila excused herself to go upstairs to the ladies' room—and indulged in some tongue display at Esther. I was left alone with her and Deronda. Ohnstad joined us.

"Hi, Danny boy. See you've fallen in with the best our party has to offer—Esther Federman and Jack Thrasher. How's Sharon Springs moving along? Have you thought of getting *I Drink Your Blood* on Turner Cable? Good fundraiser!" He laughed heartily but Deronda was silent. "I know, movies are nowhere mentioned in the Torah. By the way, Esther here has a solid grounding in the Torah. The two of you would have lots to talk about. Just for curiosity, what's your room number at the Otesaga?"

"Odd, Dr. Federman made inquiry into this matter upon our meeting," said Deronda.

"That figures. Never mind. Say, where's Sheila?"

"Ladies' room," I said.

"I must circulate," said Ohnstad, "but please let her know I asked after her. Danny, your performance was gift enough to our benefit, but I hope you have something left over for my election fund. As governor, I'll do what I can for Sharon Springs."

I ducked out and ran toward the ladies' room to find Sheila. Lots I wanted to ask her now—like why she and Esther had some mutual resentment that had eluded me, or what manner of fling she'd had with Ohnstad. What was that about sexual abuse? And, yes, did she know the whereabouts of Homero? Mother of Jesus, I hoped not.

I went up the central staircase and looked around. No Sheila. Maybe she returned to the first floor by a back stairwell. I cased the first floor. No Sheila. Then the bedrooms, the wine cellar, the servants' quarters, the fountains, frog ponds, gazeboes, treehouses, bushes, and sacred groves. No Sheila. I asked Ohnstad to make an announcement over the PA.

"Will Sheila Drake please come to the grand stairwell. Jack Thrasher awaits you."

I waited and waited. Esther and Deronda departed together in his ancient Studebaker. She was in no way concerned about her half-sister. "That slut went off with somebody else, Jack," she whispered. "Here are keys to the Mercedes. Go back to the Otesaga—take this Klonopin. And wish me well."

"I do, Esther. May the Horses of Fire be feeling their oats."

— Chapter Fifteen —

FOLLOWING HUNCHES

The Klonopin did little to ward off the dark night of the soul. Both women had left me. I assumed that down the hallway Esther was with Deronda, an improbable pickup, but for all I knew, his *yesod* might overtake her *mayim nukvim*. Maybe he was a true fiddler in bed. This was nothing like Sheila's desertion to the elephantine arms of Homero. I concluded that, yes, his absence from the benefit made it easier for Sheila to rendezvous with him afterward. I suffered visions of their doing the tango by other means. After years of abstinence she must be at the ready. It was his very incongruity that enabled her—she could be simultaneously impassioned and aloof, the fantasy made literal and held in check.

A sick and self-punishing curiosity led me to approach his room at the Otesaga. I snuck down the hall in my bathrobe and pajamas but was thwarted by three bodyguards. "Past your bedtime, chooch," said one. "Take a walk."

A late call to Sheila's cabin in Cherry Valley didn't even engage an answering machine—a contraption that interfered with natural energy lines.

Esther called me later that morning with a rundown of her night of passion with Deronda. He declined her invitation to continue the evening so that he might finish reading *Rabbi Meir of*

Rothenburg. "I'll keep trying . . . Have you heard from my sister? She doesn't answer."

"I'm surprised you even called her after yesterday's squabble," I said.

"Silly, that's how we bond. You can be really dense, Jack. But, yes, I was going to forgive her. Where is she?"

By late morning when she'd not shown up for work at the opera house, it was clear Sheila had disappeared. Esther and I went to the sheriff.

"Looky here," said Tarbox, "cain't do nuttin' fer twenty-four hours. We gotta see if she shows up dead or alive. Missing persons can already be dead, yah know. What was she wearing?"

"A fake 1860s chemise worn by Princess Hermia in the Glimmerglass production of Offenbach's *Bluebeard*," said Esther, as if this would be useful to Tarbox.

Well, it was. "Eighteen sixties," he said. "Dat's the same as when the Cardiff Giant got found. He might've took her fer one of his own. Her own fuckin' fault. Give me twenty-four hours, den I organize a search party."

Not willing to wait that long, I organized a search party of my own—Esther, Deronda, and me. At the wheel of her Mercedes, Esther took charge. In addition to a road map of Otsego County, she packed a kabbalistic primer. Off we sped, following her hunches. Deronda crouched in the backseat, terrified by Esther's lurching and screeching.

"My sister's not been kidnapped. She's making a sacred voyage, like the *yordei merkava* who descend in a chariot. *The Book of Enoch* says this voyage can last five hundred years."

"Let's try five hours, or five commercial breaks," I insisted. "I hope you're right—she just took off on her own in a snit. Where would she go?"

"Let's look at the map." She did some rapid calculations on her smartphone. "I've got it. You know of Sheila's love affair with trees. In the oral literature of Kabbalah, the word is *ilan*, from the Aramaic *ilana*. It has a gematria of ninety-one, the same as *malakh*, or angel. That's no coincidence. Now the number of love—that's *ahava* in Hebrew—is thirteen. And you know how Sheila feels about her father, quite the opposite of love. So I know where she is. She's meditating beneath a tree angel in the Forest of the Dozen Dads, purging the dad in her."

"Dozen, but you said thirteen."

"Yes, Jack, it's a baker's dozen."

So we vroomed out Black's Road to the Forest of the Dozen Dads where we found a smattering of picnic tables, a solitary family of rednecks hunkered over headcheese, and a baker's dozen of crows.

"Have you perchance seen a woman, midthirties, auburn hair, very well put together, wearing an 1860s chemise?" asked Esther of the rednecks.

The one sitting with rump hanging out over dungarees turned and replied, "Go fuck yourself, lady. Nobody here but us locals. You a kike?"

We got the message and piled back in the Mercedes. We neared Highway 33, the road to Cherry Valley.

"The sacred tree of the *sephiroth* has thirty-three branches!" exclaimed Esther. "Or maybe only thirty-two but close enough."

"And Jacob had thirty-three children by his first wife, Leah," chimed in Deronda, wishing now to ingratiate himself with Esther, a good sign.

"And Sheila's been staying in Cherry Valley," I added.

We scooted off to Cherry Valley at sixty-six miles per hour. The Cherry Valley Massacre during the Revolutionary War put the town on the map. Brits and Native Americans teamed up to murder a valley full of settlers. But it became known as "The Happy Valley" because all the survivors were high on lithium, abundant in the water supply. Sheila insisted the settlers were white imperialists, just asking for it. The Native Americans, her ancestors, were reclaiming their own.

She'd been staying on Maiden Lane in a Gothic house with steep gables and pierced bargeboards. It looked like a storybook cottage.

Put in mind of the horrors of children's literature, I knew we'd find her head on the mantle and limbs in a stewpot.

But this cottage of horrors yielded not much more than a Hall of Fame induction ceremony program signed "To Sheila—let's tango!—Tony the Bat."

Esther found relics of their girlhood days, including stuffed animals that her sister always took with her, claiming they were a more reliable source of respect and companionship than men. Next to three ceremonial peace pipes, there were also some brochures—the Lollypop Farm and Petting Zoo, the Buffalo Farm, Yogi Bear's Jellystone Park at Crystal Lake, Tepee Pete's Chow Wagon, the Fly Creek Philharmonic, the Garlic Festival at Dancing Veggie Farm, and the Erie Canal. Where to begin?

Esther set to work again on the gematriot for all these venues, while Deronda and I commiserated. "Dr. Federman's kabbalistic calculations have yet to bear fruit," he noted.

"Well, third try is charmed." But I dreaded the prospect of that petting zoo, not to mention the Fly Creek Philharmonic, so I suggested to Deronda that we figure this out with scant reference to sacred or perfect numbers. Where else might she be? My eyes then fell upon a recent issue of *The Historic Fly Creek Cider Mill & Orchard Newsletter*, lying on Sheila's straw-filled futon. It carried an ad for the *Antiques Roadshow*, now being held at Hyde Hall. Hyde Hall . . . Eureka!

"Hyde Hall! Esther, let's try Hyde Hall. I have an inkling. *Hyde* is a homonym for *hide*, as in *hiding out*. Also for buffalo *hide*, the native dress of Sheila's people."

Deronda weighed in. "Dr. Federman . . ."

"Danny, please call me Esther."

"Very well, Dr. Federman. Why don't we honor Jack's surmise and pay a quick visit? Nowhere is it written in the Torah that Sheila Drake is *not* to be found at Hyde Hall."

Deronda's special pleading swayed her. We raced down Route 20 to the northern end of Otsego Lake, over a covered bridge and through the gatehouse. There sat Hyde Hall. And just then getting out of a BMW were Ohnstad, Tarbox, Tabby, and Harris! This was a convergence, in itself a minor paranormal event.

"What are you people doing here?" I asked.

Ohnstad quickly narrated the sequence of events that brought them to the mansion. Sheriff Tarbox had reconsidered and formed a search party despite the violation of protocol. It was he who set the list of targets, largely based on where he thought the Cardiff Giant might like to drop by. First, the Ommegang Brewery, functioning memorial of the days when Otsego County produced a good percentage of the nation's hops, a thriving farm industry put out of business by Prohibition. Tarbox reasoned that the giant must have an intolerable thirst with all that dry gypsum to lug around. Maybe he and his abductee fell into a vat. The brewery's famed receptionist, a large calico cat, led the search party from room to room of painted stucco. Tarbox stood on a ladder and peered into two vats of Belgium specialty malts, offending the aged brewmaster who had insisted there were no bodies floating there. Then to the freak sideshow at the Otsego County Fair, where some of the personnel were newly hired from leftovers at the Holy Ravioli convention, including a bearded fat lady who practiced Tai Chi, imagined that she had three heads, and answered to the name of Medusa. She had asked the Holy Ravioli to remove her tattoos. Ohnstad said he hoped he was beholding a hologram, for Medusa otherwise merited a large donation of human sympathy.

"Lady, did the Cardiff Giant pass through here with one Sheila Drake, maybe lookin' fer a job?" Tarbox asked.

"You crazy? You crazy? You crazy?"

Then they were off to the Russian Orthodox monastery at Jordanville, where Tarbox asked surly questions of monks long sworn to a life of silence and sleeping on wooden beds with no mattresses. A monastery would provide convenient cover for an alien plot. No luck. Then to a balloon festival at New Berlin, where the search party boarded a hot-air balloon advertising Halliburton and tried to spot giant and maiden from the air.

Tired of these initiatives, Ohnstad suggested Hyde Hall. The *Antiques Roadshow*, just beginning a three-day gig, was settled in there. Sheila liked to pick up antiques to use as props. Maybe she wasn't missing at all.

"Not a chance," said Tarbox. "Everybody knows giants don't go ter no antique garbage heaps."

But he was outvoted, and off they went. Tarbox claimed exemption, but the rest of us prepared to pay the two-dollar cover and wait in line outside the mansion, little knowing we'd be encountering the most paranormal paranormality of them all.

— *Chapter Sixteen* —

GIRLS, INTERRUPTED

Hyde Hall isn't your typical American country mansion. Those who know say it is the finest Greek Revival structure the Northeast can boast, with fifty rooms, an elegant spiral staircase and interior courtyard, and flush toilets. You don't know right away that you're looking at so large a structure, with its squat and severe façade, all the charm of a mausoleum. Its builder, George Hyde Clarke, wished to remain an English gentleman, practicing Anglicanism and serving mutton chops to the end. His son, succeeding him, loosened his collar and gave lavish dinner parties after which the front plateau, the billiard room, and the great dining hall were festooned with snoring drunks.

Upon entering, you find to your left, an imposing drawing room and to your right, a dining hall set for twenty. People queued through these two rooms and out the portal, clutching antiques and awaiting appraisers. Among them were Tony Homero and Hazel Bouche. Homero was carrying three of his own cork-lined bats that had walloped balls out of stadiums in bases-loaded ninth innings of Game Seven in three World Series. Bouche was carrying the very voodoo pins she'd stuck into the effigy of the diva she bench-warmed for at the Met. I was relieved to find Homero there with Bouche. Yes, I was crazy, crazy, crazy.

Others schlepped polyester disco suits in powder blue, an early twentieth-century crib mattress with original tag admonition, a 1980s plastic duck decoy, a box of blue glass Noxzema jars, a crate of empty 1950s pharmaceutical pill bottles, a cargo of Burma-Shave signs, a "Draw Me" matchbook collection, and a bagful of steering-wheel knobs featuring Vargas girls.

Unlike what is edited down for broadcast on PBS, most of these locals expressed indignation at the low appraisals. "Fifty cents, if you're lucky." "Those stains in no way add to the value of the mattress." "Sorry, these Burma-Shave signs are forgeries. You can tell by the word *cow plop* rhyming with *lap top*, an anachronism." Among the items rating more than fifty cents were a Flub-a-Dub marionette in the original box, a 1924 Reed & Barton loving cup for a champion Aberdeen-Angus, and three vintage Little Black Sambo piggy banks that swallowed pennies on slices of watermelon.

The collector of steering-wheel knobs flew into a rage at the Christie's appraiser and was forcibly evicted by the *Antiques Roadshow*'s bouncer. "I think we'd have better luck in Peoria," I overheard one appraiser say.

All this I took in while Tarbox went through a homeland-security check to gain permission to search the premises. Huddled for an hour with Esther while Tabby and Harris conversed with rich Ohnstad and richer Deronda, I quietly pried out more on her early years with her half-sister. Since by now you know I'm no psychologist, their relationship had me baffled.

"Sibling rivalry? Yes, Jack, there was plenty because we competed for the occasional morsel of our father's affection. We were always ratting on each other . . . Yes, Mary Baker Eddy was behind this. She taught him to love God and not fret too much about the rotten kids . . . No, Christian Scientists see no contradiction in loving God and getting rich . . . Yes, we both came down with all the childhood diseases because he wouldn't let us get vaccinated . . . I agree, it's hard to figure why he married a Jew, then a half-breed, or why they married him, except he was rich. The moment he gained custody after my mother's death, he took me out of Hebrew School. I think he was an anti-Semite . . . No, he never mentioned my dead mother around the house. I started having dialogues with her ghost when I was ten, told Sheila about them, and she ratted on me. She was seven, old enough to know the stakes. Our father was furious, said it was an insult to my stepmother. The evil stepmother seemed to agree . . . she was always giving Sheila gifts, I was lucky to get a lump of coal . . . Traumas? Well, once I stole her Indian Barbie doll and ripped out the feathers and papoose. My stepmother caught me and whipped me good . . . Sheila hated him too—she didn't know how much at the time—but the furrier wouldn't let her have a real live kitten, only a stuffed one. She wept for a week."

At this moment an anorexic woman in her eighties wearing a floral flour sack dress cut in line. She was carrying a stuffed pheasant with a loose head and lice-eaten feathers. Her timing was good, so we didn't object. I felt a little like Thor as I resumed my interrogation, asking if Esther had anything to add to her sorry tale of the furrier father.

"Three years ago a psychic uncovered a buried memory of sexual abuse by our father when Sheila was six months old. She's still convinced of it, but this may be the only thing the ogre wasn't guilty of . . . Right, Christian Scientists don't believe in sex. He tried to convince me there was no difference between girls and boys. That was my sex education until I found out for myself with Freddy, down the block . . . Yes, in Back Bay, just around the corner from the Mother Church . . . What happened to my father? Dead by an infected hangnail. He refused treatment when it turned gangrenous, left all his money to the church—my stepmother tried to sue for her fifty percent but lost through some technicality . . . Sheila and I bonded after his death, rediscovered each other, figured out the grounds of our rivalry . . . Yes of course we have relapses, who doesn't? Those old family structures never die, they just fade away a little. Go ask Freud."

Tarbox got his search warrant. We started with the wine cellar and worked our way up—Esther, Deronda, Ohnstad, and I, with Tabby and Harris holding reality TV cameras. The sad truth about

Hyde Hall was soon obvious. The restoration was moving at such a leaden pace that the restored portions were already falling back into ruin just as the unrestored rooms were taking their turn.

Esther was getting anxious about the fate of her half-sister and was flummoxed that Kabbalah had let her down again. "I should put it to Rabbi Isaac Luria. Which of the 613 commandments did I break? Where are the *Malakhim* now that we need them?" Deronda nodded at me, signaling approval of this newfound skepticism. I nodded back.

We tried out-of-the-way places—the nut room, the butler's pantry, the laundry, the china closet, the library. No Sheila. We were getting ready to ascend the grand staircase when Ohnstad shouted, "The chapel! Let's try the chapel!" We went down the hall to the vestibule, passed the library again, and turned left. The chapel was tucked away behind the library, a carefully guarded secret at Hyde Hall because the senior Clarke had insisted in his will that nothing other than Anglicanism be practiced on the premises. Heaven forbid that a Unitarian might wander through his chapel.

The portal was covered by a large buffalo hide. Ducking under it with their cameras running, Tabby and Harris were the first in.

"Just keep doing what you're doing," they said with all the aplomb of cinema verité adepts. To whom were they speaking? I followed, then Esther, Deronda, and finally Ohnstad. We beheld a ritual in progress at the altar.

It was the support group of seven ageing county-fair beauty queens attired in their now ill-fitting coronation gowns, gathered around someone lying facedown upon the altar. This person was wrapped in another buffalo hide, with only nose, eyes, and hair showing. But it was clear that this was Sheila!

The beauty queens were chanting something that sounded like a cross between redneckese and speaking in tongues. Fourteen hands were laid on Sheila's body through the buffalo hide. At one end stood a man I remembered having spoken to briefly at the benefit. He was a convicted Enron inspirational speaker who had done his time and mastered a related skill while in prison, through the state-run occupational-rehab program. "Regression Therapy Hypnosis" is what they called it.

I began to put clues together. These folk had absconded with Sheila late in the benefit, now three days removed. I took inventory of the chapel. Yes, there was evidence of leftovers from the benefit itself—cheese-dip containers, empty bottles of Ommegang malt, German sausage tips, and other refuse strewn on the pews. The chapel was only three rooms from the larder, and other half-eaten comestibles were littered about, suggesting that what we were witnessing had been in progress for some time.

The Indian reservation gift shop had been visited—taped to the walls and hanging off the altar were replica stone pendants with turtle carvings, a sculpture of a clan mother, some baskets woven in black ash, many fake tomahawks and arrowheads, a fake bow and quiver, and some fake False Faces. And there sat Sheila's own shamanic drum.

The inspirational Enron speaker took note of the new audience, gesturing that we approach the altar. He looked like a television evangelical preacher, with slicked and dyed black hair, a plump oily pink face, and utterance so unctuous I was soon made queasy. He began beating Sheila's drum and trying to speak at the same time.

"Fellow goyim," he began, "you have entered this sacred precinct near the end of a sacred ritual. We will witness the primal rebirthing of Sherry Duke . . ."

"Sheila Drake," interjected a beauty queen.

"Ah yes, of course. Sheila Drake, who until now has been only one-quarter Heron. She will become Red Blanket Ontario, a whole Heron."

"That's Red Blanket *Orontony*," put in a beauty queen.

"Ah yes, of course, Orontony. We have worked around the clock to bring the repressed whole Heron to the surface." He beat the drum. "Red Blanket has entered her subconscious and has beheld the whole primal Heron she was as princess daughter of . . . Oratonme, the great Heron chieftain. Red Blanket has discovered that all her present issues are owing to what befell the princess in this prior life."

"Did he say *Heron*?" whispered Deronda, looking troubled. "I thought Sheila was one-quarter *Huron*. She does not look much like a bird, not to me at least."

"Well, she does have a long skinny neck," I observed.

"What befell her was this . . ." continued the man from Enron, drumming arrhythmically, "hmmm, I seem to forget what befell her . . . a prompt, please."

"Her betrothal, her betrothal," offered one of the beauty queens.

"Oh yes! She was betrothed to a great Heron warrior who demanded a dowry of ten thousand wonton."

"Doesn't he mean *wampum*?" asked Esther.

"When the chief failed to come up with the wonton, the princess was duty bound to jump off a cliff, for that was the tradition. We know this was a prior life experience because whenever Red Blanket gets too close to a man, she feels like jumping off a cliff."

"At least the princess did her traditional duty," whispered Deronda.

"Now Sherry Duke will undergo a rebirthing and come out the other end a full Heron, with the wonton she needs for total self-realization. Girls, start pushing!"

The seven faded beauty queens pushed against the birth canal of buffalo hide in the direction of Sheila's feet. I watched her chin, nose, and forehead disappear, while at the other end, her feet emerged, then her knees, groin, and belly. One of the beauty queens began dumping gallons of water from a bucket down the canal, breaking the waters, I guess.

We heard muffled gurgles from within the hide. Tabby and Harris zoomed in their cameras, knowing the ratings went up whenever lives were at stake. Ohnstad had been watching with the fidgets, and now he stepped ahead of Esther and me as we sought to intervene.

"But Mr. Ohnstad, this was your idea!" said the inspirational speaker. "Stand aside!"

The beauty queens chanted, "Push! Push! Rebirth! Rebirth!"

Sure enough, out popped Sheila from the other end of the hide. She was buck naked and, for a moment, assumed a fetal position and blinked. Then she squatted upright and shook water from her limbs like a duck.

"Hey, Sheila," said Esther, "good to have you back with us. May we fix you a nice cup of herbal tea? Does somebody have a large organic towel?"

Deronda averted his eyes from the vibrant female flesh. The seven beauty queens now laid hands on her again—and the inspirational speaker threw aside the drum, laying on his own hands for good measure. You're supposed to rub the newborn for circulation, right? But we couldn't help noting that some parts were getting rubbed more than others—so we readied for another intervention.

Suddenly, Sheila jumped up and emitted a series of *kucks*, then a loud *skyow,* and then a *skewk.*

"That's the cry of *Butorides striata*, the green-backed heron," said Deronda, a fiddler whose other avocation was bird-watching. "They feed on insects and seek out swamps and lakes."

"Let's catch her, quick," cried Ohnstad. "Tarbox, bring your net!"

They were too late, for Sheila, flapping her arms in wing beats, stretched her neck, pushed her hair into a shaggy crest, and jerked her tailbone. She snatched a large moth with her beak and swallowed, then flew out of the chapel. We chased after her down the hallway, but she eluded us, lilting across the courtyard to the stair hall. The courtyard was filled with disgruntled people showing their recently devalued family junk to one another and seeking validation. When the naked birdlike form of Sheila flew through their midst, they gawked. "Well forevermore, what's that?"

Her arms still flapping, she swooped up the vertiginous staircase to the elongated billiard room on the third floor. Hyperventilating, I too reached the billiard room, screaming "Sheila! Sheila!—please stop!" just in time to see her perched on the ironwork outside the casement. She was stretching her wings, eager to set off. As I ran toward her, her muscles tensed, she let out a final *skewk!*—and there she went, tumbling off the iron grating headfirst, her legs upright and disappearing, as my heart leapt up in astonishment and despair.

— *Chapter Seventeen* —

KNOTS UNTIED

I ran out the portico fearing what a thirty-foot vertical dive does to a human neck. There was Sheila wriggling around and flapping and still emitting *kucks*, *skyows*, and *skewks* from underneath the Alien Constraint Net.

"Nabbed her," said Tarbox. "Keep yer distance, folks. She's dangerous—yah gotta know this here is alien possession. Any exorcists?" Sheila was already surrounded by *Antiques Roadshow* rejects looking down at the naked bird-lady. Still aghast, I approached her but was beat out by Ohnstad, who knelt and cried "Sheila! Sheila! I didn't want this! Please forgive me, love!"

His pallor and dropped jaw were the equal of my own. I didn't know what he was talking about. A quick survey revealed she hadn't suffered any bruises, the discolorations being leftover poison sumac. While Ohnstad grasped one flapping hand through the net, I held on to the other and cried, "Sheila, it's Jack—come to, sweetheart, and be my love. You're a Huron, not a heron!"

The *kucks*, *skyows*, and *skewks* gradually gave way to human utterance. "Where am I? Who am I?—*skyow*—Is that you, Jack?" Then her pupils disappeared again above the whites of her eyes.

I looked up long enough to see the Enron felon shake his head and slink away.

It was fully ten minutes before Esther appeared on the scene. She was limping and her nose was bloodied. "My God! Sis—thank God you're not hurt. It's Esther!"

"Esther?—*skewk!*"

"Danny, go to the linen room and get a large muslin sheet. I was just there." When Deronda returned, he shielded his eyes and handed the sheet to Esther, who wrapped it around Sheila's naked body. This was to the dismay of Tabby and Harris, who were sending out sensational images to an international audience.

While Sheila was slowly metamorphosing from avian to hominid, Esther frowned at Ohnstad, who was trembling head to toe. "Thor, what was it the regression therapist said at the altar: 'But Mr. Ohnstad, this was *your* idea!' What's going on, Thor?"

I'd been wondering this myself. What was going on?

"Don't know what he was talking about," replied Ohnstad, looking sheepish.

"I think I know, Thor—do you recognize this?" Esther held out a piece of pale-green stationery with writing on one side and blood on the other, from her own prolific nose. I recognized Sheila's calligraphy.

Before its contents could be perused, Ohnstad grabbed it and ran off through the portico.

"Thor, yer guilty of sumpin!" shouted Tarbox, who disengaged the net from Sheila and set off in pursuit. Esther and I stayed with Sheila. Figuring she wasn't yet fully conscious and couldn't object to my use of a cell phone, I put through a 911 call. I knew that none of the hundred million live viewers would wish to get involved. Paging an ambulance was up to me.

For the next few minutes we overheard Ohnstad yelping from various casements of Hyde Hall, followed by thuds and tremors. I guessed that he was running from room to room, his large and awkward frame hitting against armoires and doors as he eluded Tarbox's Alien Constraint Net. The yelps diminished for a time, then suddenly resounded with greater force. We looked up to the iron railing off the third-story billiard room—and there was Ohnstad, perched to leap to his death. Apparently with a sense of occasion, he thought first to make some remarks to the assembly and the world. By now, CNN had a helicopter hovering to monitor the suicide.

"Before jumping, and I apologize for any mess—step aside down there!—I'd like to make a confession and explain what has driven me to this end. May I first apologize to the Farmers' Museum for—"

Before he could continue his farewell and leap to eternity, Tarbox's net overtook him and Ohnstad was dragged with little dignity into the billiard room. We could hear the pig farmer's jubilation. "Bagged him!"

Ohnstad's truncated farewell seemed enough to bring Sheila to her senses. Tying the sheet around her torso, she and the rest of us ran up to the billiard room where we found Tarbox holding the piece of stationery and standing with his foot on Ohnstad's chest, like a gladiator awaiting thumbs up or down. Ohnstad wasn't struggling; he looked resigned to a prolonged existence. But he did say, "Barry, could you please take your goddam foot off my chest? I'm not going anywhere." Tarbox declined, I assumed waiting for Tabby and Harris to catch up and send forth his fifteen minutes to the world.

It was standing room only in the billiard room as Ohnstad, under the net, tried to resume his great confession. "As I was saying, I apologize to the Farmers' Museum for—"

"Thor, before you say another word," said Esther, "let me fetch something from the sewing room. Yes, you've got some explaining to do. Danny, lend me a hand."

She limped off with Deronda, holding a kerchief to her bloody nose. Ohnstad sighed in anticipation of what they'd be lugging back. "Let them bring what they will. I'm owning up to everything."

Onlookers gasped upon the return of Esther and Deronda, and parted down the middle like the Dead Sea in *The Ten Commandments*. The two slowly transported a long gray floppy object to the front of the billiard room. At arm's length, Esther held up a large elongated smiling head while Deronda crouched behind, pushing two gigantic feet one in front of the other. The thing lumbered along like a huge shabby puppet. When they approached Ohnstad, Esther tilted the head so it would glare down at the fallen entrepreneur, who shrugged his shoulders and asked, "Anyone for a nice cup of tea?"

"I stumbled over this in the linen room running after Sheila," said Esther. "Banged up my knee and nose. Almost blacked out."

"Sorry about that, Esther," said Ohnstad. "He must have fallen off the hook."

She snatched the piece of stationery from Tarbox's mitts. "And I found *this* in a pocket of *that*." Sure enough I could see many pockets in the gray midsection of the distended puppet, as in a cargo vest.

Sheila recognized the stationery. "Esther, that's mine. Give that to me! Give it back! Gimme!" She lunged at Esther, who dodged her.

"No, Sheila, this must be read aloud to everybody!" Before my weary eyes I witnessed the regression of two professional women to teenaged sisters engaged in a smear competition. At the benefit, Sheila had ratted on Esther, and Esther now turned tables. The fright for her sister's life that she'd felt only minutes earlier gave way to gleeful taunting. But in fairness I must say that her main mission had less to do with Sheila than with Thor.

"Dear Thor, I take my pen in hand to tell you that it's all over between us. I'm sorry, but it has to be—"

"Es, stop reading!" exclaimed Sheila.

"It has nothing to do with our lousy physical relationship—"

Ohnstad grimaced. "Just get it over with, Esther."

Sheila again lunged at her sister—"Gimme that! Gimme that!"—who managed to give her the slip with help from bystanders and continued reading. "Rather, it's what my psychic has revealed to me about your character and my fatal attraction to you. This last weekend, after she did a thorough palm reading and confirmed it with tea leaves and the entrails of a mouse, she told me that you and I have no future. For one thing, Thor, if I continue with you, I'll be a male slug in my next incarnation. I'm a lover of nature, but I draw the line at male slugs—"

"She wouldn't listen when I explained that slugs are hermaphrodites," muttered Ohnstad. "This was all three years ago, folks."

By this time Sheila, once again buck naked, had overtaken Esther and was pummeling at her, while her half-sister, crouched on the floor, doggedly held on to the letter and kept reading. "But it's worse than this. My psychic has revealed to me that you are the spectral double of my father. She made me see that you may be no child abuser, you may be no furrier—but your bossy manner and nosiness make you a father figure, and that's what my inner child needs least—"

"Inner child? Lord help us," sighed Ohnstad.

"So goodbye, Thor. Please have your manservant bring over my clothes and overnight bag and the diaphragm. No hard feelings, okay? But my self-realization cries out for something more. No, don't jump to conclusions, I'm not reusing that diaphragm. The psychic says self-realization will be found in celibacy. Also that you'll have no trouble finding another woman and you should check out my half-sister, Esther. My psychic has discovered that you were Jewish in a former life. That should be enough for Esther—except for their being Jewish, she's not very choosy about men. I've decided to have no men at all. That's my path forever. All the best, your pal, Sheila."

"Not very choosy?" cried Esther indignantly. She pulled her sister's hair, to the chagrin of all enlightened feminists who happened to be watching daytime reality television. Tabby and Harris zoomed in, relieved that Sheila was naked once again. Brunette hair flew in this direction and auburn in that. Deronda and I at last separated them, I holding Sheila and he Esther around their waists. Deronda collapsed under the weight, and I took the moment to wrap Sheila up in the sheet once again.

They seemed to conclude their little sibling set-to, and they simmered down to being friends again, with just occasional pinches and tongue display, as everyone's attention once again fixed on Ohnstad. He sat up and announced that, instead of trying to get on with his confession, he would take questions.

Harris began. "You were apologizing just now to the Farmers' Museum, Thor. Are we to assume this has something to do with the Cardiff Giant, Thor? And, as a follow-up question, Thor, is this the real giant or a fake?"

"I'm glad you asked that," began Ohnstad. "Yeah, sure, this is the real giant—his gypsum has converted to muslin wrap form-fitted for aliens."

Most could not help but detect some sarcasm, but Tarbox took these words as vindication. "Yah see, yah see, it was aliens all along! I told yah so."

"Wait a minute, Barry. Just kidding. Have to tell you, I made the costume myself."

Tarbox whimpered. Ohnstad managed to sit up and continue his saga from under the net.

"Late one night in April I crept into the Farmers' Museum and applied the same stuff to the Cardiff Giant that John Browere applied to Thomas Jefferson. I poured liquid plaster over his head and feet, and told him to lie still. After thirty minutes I took off the molds and almost his ears. A perfect likeness. The rest of the costume I fashioned with methods borrowed from the Bread and Puppet Theater."

"But Thor, where's the real Cardiff Giant?" asked Tabby.

"That's easy. Just where I found him, only six feet deeper."

"Huh?"

"Yes, it confirms my view of human intelligence that nobody in all these months has thought to look *under* the open pit instead of somewhere outside it."

"You mean you dug his grave?" I asked.

"Not exactly, Sherlock. I paid others to do it for me. You're dealing with 2,995 pounds of petrified gypsum, right? I paid an additional sum to keep the gravediggers silent. Not about to name names, but I found three willing gravediggers from a neighboring agricultural county. They were vulnerable and depressed. Been out of work for many months because of regional depopulation—most of the local baby boomers are already dead and buried from eating lard and wieners."

"But why? Why'd you do it?" asked Esther.

We were surely getting to the heart of the matter.

"That's not so easy. Have you got a few minutes? This may take a detour into my early life."

A hush spread through the billiard room as everyone cupped ears toward Ohnstad. More given to elliptical utterance, he shifted to an oratorical grand style I'd not heard from him before.

"Like Jack Thrasher here, I was born a Midwesterner, St. Paul, but blue collar. Parents were Lutheran underclass drudges. My father worked as janitor of the Masonic Lodge and chaffed at his lot. He got even by divulging the Masonic diaper ritual to outsiders and secretly soiling the diapers with gravy just minutes before Masonic funerals. My mother made the gravy. I'm not sure what else she did in life apart from the additional spawn of brothers and sisters with whom I had little truck. My peers at school made fun of me because everything was out of proportion—my knees didn't go with my legs, my ears were too big for my nose, my teeth too large for my mouth, my face was too long for my head, and my words too long for my age."

Esther butted in. "All of this is still true, Thor."

"Feeling like a teenaged creature from the Black Lagoon, I sought refuge in philosophy and discovered the great Enlightenment figures—Voltaire, Diderot, Hume. The more I looked into my own religion, the more its god seemed to take pleasure in my pain. And no matter how many times I helped old ladies with grocery bags, I knew I'd end up in hell if this were God's pleasure in the matter. I began to think God was little improvement over Vlad the Impaler."

There was some squirming among onlookers at this heady excursion into theology. I thought to keep Ohnstad on track. "Sorry to interrupt, Thor, but you've got to hurry and tie this in with digging a grave for the Cardiff Giant. CNN will call off its reporters!"

"I'm getting there, Jack, hold on. Since there was no premium in the eyes of God on good works, and no girl would go out with me, I pondered life's options, including suicide, and decided I might as well put money in my purse. Got into the Wharton School on scholarship and the rest is history. I made a fortune in junk bonds before the collapse and survived an SEC inquiry. This was my class revenge—I talked rich Ivy League grads into buying those bonds, ruining them. Then I set up as a country gentleman. Bought the Busch Mansion, went to the opera one evening, and by chance met Sheila Drake. This was my undoing."

Sheila smiled and wriggled her head to and fro as if laying claim to unbridled power over men. Ohnstad stared at her resignedly from under the net.

"If you don't mind, pet, I'll speak of you in the third person." He then addressed the larger company. "I prefer not to wax maudlin but must say that Sheila and I seemed to find a love beyond the ordinary, one neither of us had known. She had dated scores of pea-brained macho-narcissists from schools of the performing arts. She mistook their vacuous silences for a deeply felt and admirable reserve. To the extent I'd had relationships, I was loved only for my money—that is, not at all. Sheila was different. Or seemed to be."

"I'll admit, Thor, you were a cut above my other boyfriends. You could talk."

"But Sheila's passion for me coincided with her jumping off the deep end."

"Deep end?" I asked.

"Yes, into every New Age racket that came along. At first I played along, going with her to a dowsers' convention, for example. There I learned that dowsing doesn't just mean finding well water. You can dowse a bottle of vitamin E—in fact you've *got* to dowse vitamin E and everything else you get at a discount drugstore. This was time-consuming but nowhere near the time it took to find natural, organic foodstuffs not contaminated by West Nile virus spray. We had to drive to an organic produce farm in Canajoharie County. Then she decided she had multiple chemical sensitivity and was nearly fired by the Glimmerglass when she refused to paint the sets. Happily, non-toxic turpentine in vast quantities saved the day. But then she fell in with pyramid worship and said we'd cease having sex until she could build a pyramidal canopy out of weighted flats from the opera. She thought it a bad omen when the canopy collapsed during rear entry. I was never treated to that posture again."

Esther laughed, but Sheila didn't look pleased with any of this.

Ohnstad's interminable confession took a more interesting turn. "Now I must talk about human psychology—alas, my own." He breathed deeply, as did I. "After the psychic of Butternuts County convinced Sheila to dump me and shun the company of men, I was unhinged. It was grief. Grief is a craving, and I craved her. I'd sneak backstage at the Glimmerglass disguised as a woman but was quickly outed by her colleagues. I'd drive to Cherry Valley and lay siege to her cottage but my BMW was a giveaway. I sent her organic yellow roses but they ended up on my own doorstep with 'Return to Sender.' Occasionally she'd consent to lunch at the Blue Mingo Grill, but it was as if I were dining with a long-lost second cousin thrice removed. We no longer had anything in common. And she wouldn't let me speak—how shall I say it?—the discourse of the heart."

"What's dat, Thor?" asked Tarbox, tightening the net.

Ohnstad ignored him. "My grief and blunted passion then bore stranger fruit. How to explain this? Well, one consequence you can grasp easily enough. I swore vengeance on the paranormal—on every superstitious practice that could waylay honest human relationships or convince people they're something they're not or put aside all rules of evidence in favor of bogus miracles. These miracles suspend the natural order so that any rube working the nightshift at Kmart can feel he's at the center of things. The universe changes its ways to make an impression on him, *on him*! The impoverished egos of alien abductees inflate to the orbit of Jupiter. It's an identity thing. What an honor to be singled out by aliens!"

"This is all very eloquent, Thor, but what's this have to do with the Cardiff Giant?" I asked.

"That should be obvious, sport. I wanted to make lots of people pay for their gullibility. They'd all be taken in. There'd be a big commotion—hey, good for local business—and everybody would stick out necks with explanations. Aliens, Druids, the golem—what horseshit! Second time around, this Cardiff Giant hasn't lost any of its power to bamboozle. I made some timely appearances to reinforce the hysteria—the Glimmerglass Opera, Sharon Springs, Gilbert Lake—sorry guys—but, as I correctly guessed, I could just sit back and 'evidence' of paranormal events would spread like wildfire. Sabotaging the Hall of Fame ceremony was lots of fun, gotta say. Then my plan was to confess the hoax—embarrassing an entire world of fools now that the giant's disappearance has been reported in Beijing and Singapore. Maybe I'd even win some converts to the rational side of things. That at least was my agenda. Wishful thinking, you say? Okay, I confess I've been working more out of bile than indignation. So now I've done it, confessed the hoax. Oh, almost forgot the Holy Ravioli—made it myself—same principle as Browere's life masks but I used pasta instead of plaster and modeled it on a dashboard Mel Gibson. Guess I'll see if my master plot works from inside a jailhouse."

"If yer lucky," said Tarbox. "Yah might get lynched instead. Think I'll just hand yah over ter the voters. We use ter have a gallows next ter the river."

"Thanks, Barry. But please remember I treated you to kir and larger bribes over the years. So folks, it turns out I'm just as gullible, just as crazy as the next nut," said Ohnstad. "I learned this the hard way. I thought if I couldn't have Sheila up close, I'd have her at a distance. For three years behind the scenes, I tried to fix her up with other men, thinking I could spy on them at the local ice cream parlor. Maybe she'd be seducible, and I'd get a vicarious kick. Yes, there was also an element of revenge, on her and the psychic—maybe I could undo their celibacy pact. And yes, if she were to break the vow once, maybe I could move in again and she'd take me back. See, no singleness of motive—a convergence. So I sent widowers, composers, botanists, vegetarians, veterinarians, athletes, and even a journalist or two her way." He looked at me ruefully. "These suckers would ask to see her on pretexts not having to do with dating or romance, and sometimes she consented. I'd feel a strange surge of desire and repulsion whenever I thought she might be yielding to overt advances. You call this sick? I agree."

Sheila started sticking a billiard cue at Ohnstad under the net. "Yes, sick, sick, sick! Take that! And that! Pimp!"

Now I began to see how Ohnstad was my double as well as my nemesis. I suffered similar torments of love, jealousy, and envy when I imagined that Homero was making it with Sheila. There was all that "evidence"—the tango, the handkerchief, the signed Hall of Fame program, the weird praise she heaped on the jerk, and Ohnstad's insinuations. It all seemed to point to Homero. Wasn't my sex nausea caused by *something*? Well, the alien abductees had their evidence, I had mine. In truth, none at all.

Here's the check from the mind's deep emotive spring on the rationalist's presumption. Ohnstad was heir to Enlightenment skepticism yet had become unhinged by passion, and his war against the paranormal was itself grounded in insanity—no deeper irony. I liked to think of myself as somebody whose mind wasn't so made up, a reporter who followed the evidence. It was fun when the evidence pointed to the reanimation of the Cardiff Giant. It was no fun at all when the evidence insisted that Sheila was getting it on with Homero. Now I saw that both these delusions were simply absurd. The question became how in the future to be wise, and here I wasn't sure.

"But why the rebirthing? The regression hypnotist said that was all *your* big idea," said Esther. "Did you kidnap my sister, creep?"

"I wouldn't call it kidnapping, but yes, I arranged for the county beauty queens and regression hypnotist to seduce her, as it were. Here again, with your forgiveness, I must indulge some psychology. Sheila Drake's psychic had convinced her that she was a full-blooded Huron in a previous life. It gave me a rush to think I might be the one who fulfilled her grand illusion—who restored her own identity to herself. Somehow I imagined I would get the credit. And if she really believed she'd purged the non-Huron, the furrier father part, maybe she and her goddam psychic would stop identifying me with this father—and

I could step in once again." He continued, his voice trembling with shame and contrition. "You see how fine reasoning can be put into the service of dementia! Yes, I confess I was demented. And it got out of hand. They nearly killed the girl. That hypnotist either had a lousy memory or was hard of hearing—I *know* I told him to rebirth her as a Huron, not a heron. Details, details. Really sorry about that, Sheila."

"*You're* sorry!" She jabbed and jabbed.

"She has a point," I said.

"Yes, we must learn to speak for ourselves, John—I mean Jack. I was off in a realm of my own, inhabited by chimeras no less fantastic than Esther's kabbalistic angels. I could still cast stones on superstition. But it's a bit humbling. I remember what an English essayist said about his own sexual jealousy, 'I am in some sense proud that I can feel this dreadful passion'—Ouch! Lay off, Sheila, I've paid my dues."

By now the media and others were clearing out because Ohnstad's explanation was far too complicated for a daytime television audience. Tarbox put handcuffs on him and read him his rights, not badly for someone who could barely read. The charge was "impersonating an alien." The sheriff led the impersonator down the stairwell to the paddy wagon just as the ambulance arrived, an hour late because the driver took a shortcut. I told the medics that the bird-lady was fully recovered, if not covered. We looked for where the rebirthers had put Sheila's *Bluebeard* chemise. As it turned out, it was on the hook in the sewing room next to Ohnstad's Cardiff Giant costume. He had not gone to great lengths to conceal his costume, trusting once again that people wouldn't see the obvious. Well, unlike Bluebeard, he didn't slit any throats but he almost broke one, and in this chamber he had hung his dark secret.

As he was climbing into the paddy wagon, Ohnstad smiled. "By the way, Esther, you'll find that copy of the Zohar in the library—hate to tell you, it doesn't glow in the dark."

— Chapter Eighteen —

SOFT LANDINGS

With Ohnstad disposed of, we all scooted to the library. There, wedged between *The Last of the Mohicans* and *Zen and the Art of Motorcycle Maintenance*, we found the Zohar. Esther and Deronda lugged the volume to the reading table and opened it to the frontispiece.

"Uzziel Deronda, Far Rockaway, August 12, 1946," read Deronda, squinting.

"Mordechai Federman, Rockaway, August 12, 1946," read Esther. "Yes, they signed the same day—they must have been friends and neighbors. We've got lots in common, Danny. Let's take it to the linen closet and see if it glows in the dark."

Ohnstad was right again. No glow. We all sat down at the reading table as if we were at a pro-seminar.

Silence for quite some time. Then Esther sighed. "Guys, I've been rethinking *The Kabbalah of Everyday Life*. Hope you'll understand if I tell you I'm giving the whole thing up. I've calculated the number of times gematrias and repairing vessels have got me in trouble since the giant disappeared. I should have guessed," she laughed, "the number is perfect: twenty-eight."

"Well, you do have that class action suit to worry about," I said— my polite Midwestern way of encouraging her in this new way of thinking.

"But, sis," said Sheila, "what'll you put in its place? It's hard to imagine you without your seraphim and chariots and husks . . ."

"Not to mention your voyage of sparks and column of harmony and horses of fire," I added.

"Somehow I used to get along without them. Look at Madonna. She was doing well enough before she took a course at the Kabbalah Center."

"Excuse me," said Deronda, abruptly. "I must call my mother." Glancing at Sheila, he added, "I shall make use of the public phone." He was gone for ten minutes, during which Esther lamented Rabbi Isaac Luria's flop at resolving life's daily vexations. "I may have another look at Freud too, while I'm at it. What's *he* good for?"

Deronda returned and stood at the end of the table. He removed his glasses and, with a sense of occasion, solemnly asked, "Dr. Federman, would it be inappropriate at this hour if I were to ask you to marry me?"

"Not at all. I accept!"

She leapt to embrace Deronda, almost knocking him over. Sheila expressed pleasure at this outcome, offering right away to serve as maid of honor, and I accepted Deronda's invitation to serve as best man.

I'll scope ahead. The couple lived happily ever after. Having given up Kabbalah and losing the class action suit and her license to practice psychoanalysis, Esther switched to social work, taking her MSW at NYU and focusing on ageing Jewish communities below the poverty line in the Bronx. She served as accounts manager of a Jewish burial society and saw to it that all decedents got down under within twenty-four hours. She became a cantor much praised for her warmth of voice and impeccable Hebrew. And she assisted Deronda in his lifework of restoring Sharon Springs. The results can be smelled to this day.

Living in other respects high off the hog on Park Avenue, the couple had a daughter named Rachel. They packed her off at an early age to the Rodeph Sholom Hebrew School. Rachel's first combination of words was "Yay! Temple!" Fired by the Discovery Channel for letting Tabby and Harris get the upper hand in the Cardiff Giant story, I slunk back to the city a few days after the events at Hyde Hall to look for work. I undertook to revive the *East Village Other*, a fringe newspaper from the sixties, and quickly gained a readership of old-timers still committed to print culture. A year passed and in the early fall I boarded a bus to Cooperstown, where I called on Sheila at the Glimmerglass Opera. She was already working on sets and costumes for the next summer's new production of *Lizzie Borden*. "Jack, what a surprise!" She was wearing baggy Levi's and a baggier Irish sweater.

She suggested we take a walk down through the Goodyear Swamp Sanctuary, directly behind the opera house. I feared another encounter with the Plant Spirit Underworld but readily agreed. We walked down the steep path toward Otsego Lake, pausing at the water view station. Along the way we passed many trees—speckled alder, buckthorns, winterberries—but I noticed she didn't speak to any of them, not even the swamp maples. At first I thought maybe it was just that, with a path so obviously marked, she didn't need to ask directions.

Looking toward the lake, we saw a great blue heron standing in full majesty at the water's edge. She watched it for many minutes through binoculars, then said, "Jack, I've changed. Something happened after that plunge I took off the railing."

"Tell me about it, if you like. What's different?"

"One difference is I'm a student again. Taking two adult ed courses in this sanctuary. It's run by the SUNY Oneonta biology department and has two hundred species of vascular plants. A great place to learn botany and field biology."

"But I thought you already knew botany. What's happened with your Plant Spirits?"

"It's hard to explain. A eureka moment a few days after you left. I saw there's nothing more miraculous than a Jack-in-the-Pulpit. Here's one."

Jack? I liked where this was going. I had always liked my jaunty nickname.

She bent down to inspect a cluster of red berries on the plant of about two feet. "There's so much to learn about this plant, *Arisaema triphyllum*! It's also called Indian turnip. This one could be a hundred years old. You know it begins life as a male, then becomes a female, then becomes a male again, then a female."

"Can't make up its mind?" I asked.

Sheila laughed—already something new in her approach to plants. "No, dumb bunny, it depends on starch. Every season the flower decides whether it'll be male or female. Depends on how much starch it's stored in its corm. The more starch, the more likely it'll be female. It takes more energy to be female, and the plant prefers to be female, in the interest of species reproduction. The males are only temps, servicing the females."

"Sounds like George Bernard Shaw. Wasn't it his Don Juan in Hell who said only females are in grips of the life force, while males just make their screwy little donation?"

"Yes, the life force in action late in the season. These berries have replaced the flowers of early spring. Remarkable flowers. Large, three-lobed leaves hang over the spathe . . . looks like a pulpit or hood. And inside the spathe is a bulb—the spadix or *jack*."

"I don't mean to sensualize this," I replied, "but I know something of the lore. Isn't it a toss-up whether a Jack-in-the-Pulpit resembles a hooded clitoris or an uncircumcised penis?" Okay, I meant to sensualize this.

"My Huron ancestors ground up the roots to enhance potency. But I take a larger view of this plant—plants are allegories, not spirits. Every plant has a story. When I called on the Plant Spirit of Jack-in-the-Pulpit, just to stay in practice, I got no answer. Made me think of cell phones that don't work just when you need them."

"Cell phones!"

"Don't worry, I've not gone that far to the other side. But in these botany courses I've found a different way of communicating with plants."

"You mean science?"

"Well yes, sort of." She hesitated. "Let me tell you more about these Jacks-in-the-Pulpit. You know how the female flower gets pregnant?"

"The usual method?"

"With variations. You've got to have fungus gnats carry the pollen from male flowers to female. But they do so at a price. The poor gnats are fooled by the smell of the plant—it's like the fungi where they normally lay their eggs."

"So deception lays the ground for reproduction? Sounds all too human."

"Yes, the gnats jump to conclusions. When they fly into the male pulpit, they're trapped for a time and beat about, picking up pollen. There's a slit at the bottom of the male pulpit, so many get free just to fly into a nearby female pulpit."

"Doesn't she have an escape slit too?"

"No, the female is slitless."

"Hmmm . . . a real variation."

"Yes, the poor gnats are trapped forever, but it means they are more likely to transfer the pollen. The female gets pregnant and the flower turns into what we see here—a bright-red berry full of seeds."

"So the ends of nature are served. Those poor fungus gnats must feel used. It's so unethical. I guess that's what Darwin was telling us all along about nature . . . But why does this dark allegory cheer you up?"

"Because there's more meaning in it than my Plant Spirits. They were supposed to be friendly and generous, sacrificing themselves to help us out like Shmoos. But how to explain the poison sumac? I felt let down by plants, like Esther felt let down by Rabbi Isaac Luria. Now this Jack-in-the-Pulpit is poisonous too if you rub up against it. And ruthless with those gnats. Learning about it—the things that are beautiful, the things that are scary, the things that seem human, the things that aren't at all human—all this made me see the flower as a miracle, but . . ."

"Wholly within the natural order?"

"Exactly—the Jack-in-the-Pulpit has its own reasons for doing things the way it does, its own causes, like other flowers, but different too. It made me want to find out the real story behind every plant—but there are so many! I've got my hands full just with this sanctuary."

We continued down to the boarded walkway over the swamp. "All this purple loosestrife," she said. "Very pretty herbaceous plant but it crowds out the rushes and burreeds."

"Imperialistic?"

"Yes, another unfriendly plant with a story to tell."

Our approach scared off the heron. I wasn't about to bring up the question of Huron identity and how much depends on spelling and pronunciation. But she did.

"You know, Jack, I almost got killed because a professional rebirther didn't know the difference between *Huron* and *heron*. It made me rethink this whole pursuit of identity and lots of other New Age stuff. Bet you'll be happy to hear I've decided to accept the identity I've got—just one-fourth Huron. That's enough, because I'm other things as well. A first-rate set and costume designer, a student of botany, a part-Irish woman who is . . ." She trailed off.

"Possessed of passion, beauty, and intellect." Again I'd finished a sentence for her. Masculinist!

"Thanks for that. Maybe I was going to say 'alive and well.' I don't think I've told you how touched I was when Esther told me all about your search party and how worried you were. What brings you here now, Jack?"

"It has to do with identity too. Yours and mine together. Is there a chance?"

She took my hand and gave it a squeeze. "Let's try."

Hand in hand, we strolled along the walkway toward the lake access, prompting green frogs to leap for cover. We paused near a family of forget-me-nots and hog peanuts with their purplish-green flowers in full bloom. Here we exchanged our first kiss, hesitant, non-invasive, full of promise.

"Yes, let's try," I said.

I'll scope forward again. The courtship was slow and given to moments of mutual doubt, but I earned her trust. Maybe it was that I'm a fraternal, not paternal, sort of male—and that set me apart from her father and Ohnstad.

We eventually married. She had enough starch in her corm and I enough pollen in my pulpit to produce three offspring. We made no use of fungus gnats. As I write, we are all living happily ever after in a condo on Tompkins Square, overlooking where Abbie Hoffman first draped himself in the American flag.

You may remember that in the beginning I was nothing, a man without qualities except for a certain comic perspective on things. I arrived in Cooperstown with a nearly blank slate. There's something in our wiring that's unsatisfied with nothing—and I wanted things to happen, to fill that slate. They did, and I found myself in a plot concocted by another—Thor Ohnstad and his revenge on gullibility. He saw himself a victim in his dealings with Sheila. This was mixed up with his sick vicariousness, this pimp of human souls. I escaped, just barely, and learned that one must seek out what one wants, speak for oneself, make things happen. I fell in love and suffered the jealous delusions of love, almost becoming Ohnstad.

But on the other side of a dark rite of passage, I took an Adirondack Trailways bus and asked Sheila to marry me. In our domestic love I felt that slate being filled in.

Our persons aren't isolable bundles of traits—we are plural, with permeable boundaries. Who was I now? The Jack Thrasher who lives with Sheila and pitches in with the kids and shares friends and does journalism.

But I should tell you the fate of Ohnstad and the others in my small cast out of central casting. It was like Dante's *Inferno*, where punishment is meted out that matches the crime. After a night in the Cooperstown jail, when Sheriff Tarbox took revenge by locking him up with three pigs, Ohnstad pleaded guilty to all charges before a county magistrate. Sentenced to daily AA meetings, he was obliged to pledge allegiance to a Higher Power. And he was sentenced to 496 days of community service, consisting of custodial work at the Farmers' Museum. This meant a daily cleaning of the Cardiff Giant, again exhumed, and of latrines at Bump Tavern, a 1795 structure moved from Windham, New York, to the Farmers' Museum, its odor of urine and tobacco intact. He was forced to serve as clerk with no salary at the museum's general store and to attend Sunday services and sing hymns at the country church, hoisted to the museum from Cornwallville, New York. Had to spend nights at the unaccommodating Seneca Log House, with its bed of scratchy straw.

Ponder also what happened to Bouche and Homero. For her stubborn trust in astrology, she was forbidden to sing at the Met or La Scala. Too many audiences had thrown tantrums instead of tantra, too many people cancelled subscriptions. But Bouche grew only more stubborn in her horoscope and, by golly, she prevailed. The horoscope led her to a chat room where she hooked up with a television Southern Baptist evangelical and—you know the rest. She gave up Gounod for Gospel, uncovered her roots, and belted out the Gospel sound to millions on cable while her husband, a black Oral Roberts, chalked up more cures than the Holy Ravioli could ever boast. They lived happily ever after.

Homero? Hard to believe I ever feared he was shtupping Sheila. This is enough to remind us that the skeptical temper with respect to matters normal and paranormal doesn't always keep the yellow demons at bay. For all our gray matter, we live in a world of illusion. And we may fail in matters of the heart. But Homero too prevailed in the end and, as I write, is living happily ever after. He pined so much on the steps of the Baseball Hall of Fame that the baseball commissioner reconsidered, and after ample consultation with his Ouija board, admitted Homero. Go read the plaque. But for Homero, baseball was remote history. He bailed also from the scaffolding business and, with some venture capital, started the now famed Homero Tango Institute, which holds annual international tango competitions attended by celebs the world over. The HTI Table Top Tango trophy is particularly treasured.

Tarbox simply disappeared one day.

Life in the city has been good for us two couples and kids. Sheila gave up her position at Glimmerglass for the same work as designer at the Metropolitan Opera. She and Esther get together for lunch every three weeks or so, often at the Boathouse in Central Park, where they watch the swans and rowboats and ponder everything from child-raising and discount drugstores to botany and Jewish burials. They rise above the petty sibling jealousies I've documented with some embarrassment in this history. I can't say I've become close to Deronda, who doesn't get my jokes, but I respect his doggedness and enterprising nature as well as his extraordinary fiddling. His klezmer bluegrass suggests to me a deep truth about how human beings can contain contradictory multitudes, often latent powers that well up on occasion, surprising, ennobling.

My newspaper focuses on urban-environment issues but has a weekly supplement devoted to cosmology and astrophysics. Far from emulating Ohnstad's skepticism with respect to all matters beyond experiment and direct observation, I've made my compromise with Sheila and Esther, who seek a spiritual dimension in things—often, as we've seen, at their peril. I've taken up integral yoga and dine once a month with Sheila at Souen, a macrobiotic restaurant. Because it doesn't believe in disinfectants, Souen is often closed down by the Department of Health but always gets back in business.

It's really in cosmology where I find a spiritual turn of the screw. The *East Village Other* is so taken up with garbage removal, rent stabilization, urban blight, and ozone that, in my editor's column, I like to remind the readership of worlds elsewhere. I discovered cosmology many years ago while reading *Einstein in Love*, which I had mistaken for an account of the scientist's sex life. There was little on sex but much on how mind at its highest pitch begins to understand the cosmos. If our blue dot in space becomes opaque in time through the greenhouse effect or some other human malfeasance, there's the consolation that this particular universe of at least 125 billion galaxies must contain planets that are doing a better job of it. This stands to reason, though there's no direct evidence. The unfathomable infinity of space, the unspeakable stretch of time, the wonder of the firmament—all answer to whatever vestige I have of a sense of the miraculous. And much of it is spooky too, like the demise of one photon linked to the demise of another, even if they are whizzing off toward different galaxies.

Bertrand Russell once opined that philosophy is that branch of speculation that hasn't yet been replaced by science. Okay, Bertie, but in cosmology we find science still engaged in speculation, trying to explain a huge amount of resistant stuff.

So what's the difference between cosmology and a belief in the paranormal? Tough question—and don't expect a convincing answer from a mere journalist when Carl Sagan couldn't come up with one. But consider human presumption: Cosmologists, unlike the horoscope gang, don't imply it all exists for our sake—we're not sure where we stand in the nature of things. And cosmologists reluctantly say goodbye to their incandescent theories if Mother Nature extinguishes them with the wet blanket of counter-evidence.

* * *

One day in October, ten years after the events of 2003, the four of us were invited by Ohnstad, on elegant hotel stationery, to spend the weekend at the Otesaga, at his expense and for old time's sake—and Deronda should bring his fiddle. We hadn't seen him in years. There was some debate as to whether we should accept, but curiosity got the better of us, and we left the kids with nannies. What did Ohnstad have up his sleeve this time? Do people ever truly reform? He had long since finished his community service gig at the Farmers' Museum and given up all hope of higher office. For all we knew he was simply minding his accounts and settling into wealthy, corpulent late middle age.

We drove up to Cooperstown in Deronda's refurbished Duesenberg, no longer a Studebaker, with Esther at the wheel driving in her customary manner—turning a four-hour journey into three-with Deronda as usual cowering in the backseat.

Have you noticed that this screed has been a meditation on identity? I can safely say that some things never change about the people we know, from preschool to the grave. Esther will always be a reckless driver, just as she must have been a reckless toddler.

We were to meet in a pavilion erected for the occasion behind the hotel. Leaving the limousine in the parking lot, we walked through the portico and out the lobby to the expansive porch behind, overlooking the lake where the phantoms of Cooper's novels flit about at night. Some thirty yards below was a newly erected pavilion, modeled on the exhibition tent of 1869 that had first housed the Cardiff Giant. Hotel staff were scurrying to and fro, toting champagne and hors d'oeuvres into the pavilion entrance. From a distance we could see an unusually tall woman standing at the entrance, bossily instructing them.

"Ohnstad seems to have hired an Amazonian social director," I whispered to my three companions as we approached the pavilion.

"Sheila! Esther! Jack! Danny! Wasn't expecting you for another hour—I've hardly had time to fix my face!" She was wearing a long scarlet gown, décolleté with sequins, and high heels, as if she weren't already tall enough.

"Sorry, where is Mr. Ohnstad?" I asked, puzzled that this stranger was already addressing us by first names. There was something uncanny about her. I did a quick inventory of her long horsy face. The women beat me to it.

"Thor! It's you!" they cried simultaneously.

"Wanted you to be the first to know, dearies," said Ohnstad. "Took many surgeries and lots of hormones, but how do you like my new look?"

"You look great!" said Esther.

"A real improvement, Thor," said Sheila. They both gave him a hug.

I thought he looked like a female Seabiscuit but held my tongue.

"Call me Arlene," said Ohnstad.

"So you've invited us up for the coming-out?" I asked. "We're honored, Thor—I mean, Arlene."

"Yes, but it's more than that, lovelies. I'm announcing my engagement. You'll meet him shortly. Let's catch up first. Dario, do bring the champagne tout de suite, and hurry up with the hors d'oeuvres, s'il vous plait." She snapped her fingers.

Other guests were arriving. We may have been in Arlene's inner circle but this was a public festival. Sure enough, setting up cameras at the far end of the pavilion were Tabby and Harris with their crew, ten years older than when we last saw them. Harris had the same oily hairpiece and Tabby the same face-lift, maybe three times re-upholstered—and both had the same Chiclets and receding gums. I repeat, some things abide the flux of time.

"Let's face it," began Arlene when we'd rounded up chairs and settled down into yet another pro-seminar, "I wasn't very good at being a man . . . so I surveyed the alternatives."

I wondered if he—no she—had been eating lots of starchy foods.

"Spending a night in jail with three pigs made me think I'd taken a wrong turn somewhere."

"Yes, many wrong turns, like getting involved with me," said Sheila. "You know, Arlene, I've had some bad feelings about listening to that psychic and calling the whole thing off. But you know, I don't think it was going to work out anyway. Sorry you got so unhinged over it, obsessing and siccing other guys on me. That was as crazy as my thinking I was a heron."

"I agree, dear," said Arlene. "I was a textbook case in abnormal psychology and you were in a hypnotic trance. But I must say, it worked out in the long run. Look here at Jack—you owe him to me, dear. At least I get some of the credit, don't I, Jack?"

"Not sure I get *any* of it," I replied. "You get the credit, Arlene, but I'm not sure what you're going to do with it."

"I'm investing in the future," she replied flatly.

It had long ago occurred to me that Ohnstad's crazed revenge on the paranormal had borne some fruit despite his exposure and defeat in the end. Esther had backed away from Kabbalah for mainstream Judaism and Sheila had renounced baloney for botany. Deronda and I had stepped in where Ohnstad had trod, both of us living happily ever after. Surely he had some entitlement to a future.

"So what's in the cards?" I asked her.

"For starters, meet my fiancé." She snapped her fingers.

We were promptly joined by a stout, presentable late middle-aged man wearing a costly, rumpled, dark linen suit and a silk tie with an animalist motif. He was sipping a kir.

"Haven't we met somewhere before?" I asked. I peered into eyes that peered into mine as in a dream many years ago. Again, the women beat me to it.

"Tarbox!" they cried simultaneously. "You've changed!"

"Good evening, ladies," said Tarbox. "Yes, I've changed, thanks to Arlene here. She put me through an extreme makeover. Those *Queer Eye for the Straight Guy* guys showed up one day. Then lots of plastic surgery, new duds, speech lessons, I sold my pigs, lost the election, learned how to read and tango, changed my politics. Now I'm doing work on the net."

"Oh, you're still catching aliens?" I asked. "I'm so grateful to you for catching Sheila with that net."

"No, the *worldwide* net. I gave up on aliens long ago and took up fishing. Me and Arlene met through the Cooperstown Dating Service."

"But you'd already been doing business together for years," I observed.

Arlene raised her left eyebrow. "Yes, lovelics, but neither of us knew with whom we were dealing. When we met up at the Blue Mingo Grill, we had a good laugh. Of course I'd gone through my own extreme makeover by then and was forced to tell Barry who I was. I was still eight inches taller."

"Me and Arlene—uh, I mean, Arlene and I hit it off," said Tarbox. "I was disappointed at first 'cause she didn't know how to can."

"But I reminded him that I had ample funds," said Arlene, "and we really wouldn't need to lay in provisions for the winter months."

"So will your name be Arlene Tarbox?" Deronda asked Ohnstad.

"No, I got my name changed," interjected the former pig farmer.

"Yes, meet Baron Turbot," said Arlene. "My name will be Arlene Ohnstad-Turbot. Let me tell you more about all this, if you're interested. With your permission, Esther, I must dip into abnormal psychology yet again. Baron has already heard all this, but no matter."

"Please, Arlene," said Esther. "We're all ears."

"Very well, lovelies. You'll remember I was quite undone by Sheila's giving me walking papers on advice of that psychic."

"Don't rub it in."

"And then I fell into trying to make love to her by proxies, blokes like you, Jack."

"Pardon my own psychology," interjected Esther, "but maybe it was your way of dealing with loss and jealousy—you were still in charge. Not so odd, really."

"Remember, you're a control freak," Sheila added.

"Okay, okay. But it felt odd. I was aroused by my jealousy . . ."

"Prurience and castration go hand in glove," pitched in Esther. "I think Freud has something on that somewhere."

"But what I've not confessed is that I was identifying with Sheila, not with the men, seeing these male invaders from the female point of view. It was arousing. I tried to take up residency in her body. In my mind's eye, that is." Arlene hadn't fully worked out some voice-pitch issues and was going back and forth irritatingly between falsetto and basso.

She continued, "After my exposure and disgrace at Hyde Hall—"

"Don't forget my pigs."

"Yes, and after conversing in jail with Baron's three castrated pigs, I pondered who I was. I couldn't walk down the street anywhere without people pointing and saying things like 'There goes the pervert!' or 'How's life at the Farmers' Museum, Mr. Ohnstad?' or 'Serves you right, goddam atheist.' I thought of growing a beard, changing my name and hair color, and moving to another part of the country. Then I hit on a sex change. Maybe I was all along a woman trapped in a man's body."

Arlene caught my eyes rolling. "Yes, Jack, it's a cliché but no less true for that."

Okay, I could grant the occasional truth of clichés. And frankly, it seemed doubly confirmed by now that the psychic had been right to warn Sheila away from Ohnstad. I remembered too that his obsession with her had become my own, like an infection. I had felt the dark arousal of envy and jealousy and their assault on my identity. I had been in a delusional state of mind.

Well, there was one difference between Ohnstad and me—I had never taken up residence, in thought or deed, in a female body. Guess I'm an unregenerate hetero.

"Now, Arlene," said Esther, knowing she might be raising a sensitive issue, "what was there about Baron that was so compelling? Not that he doesn't cut quite a figure on the dance floor, but, uh . . ." This was, of course, a question lurking in all our minds. I must say that neck-flap reduction, jowl and double-chin removal, rhinoplasty, hair implants, and a tummy tuck had done wonders for this pig farmer. Still, who would've thunk it? Ohnstad's making do with Tarbox could not have been flattering to Sheila and Esther, former girlfriends now scratching their heads.

"I felt we deserved each other," said Arlene and left it at that. "Now, if you'll excuse us, lovelies, we should say hello to some of our other guests." She lumbered off while Baron Turbot waddled beside her. Those walks, at least, hadn't changed for the better.

I surmised—and Esther later agreed—that courting Tarbox must have been some sort of self-flagellation. But whatever his motives, Ohnstad had gone to work on this unpromising pig farmer and refashioned him. I repeat, people never completely change their identities despite all this talk of reinvention. Any particular Jack-in-the-Pulpit switches sex depending on its annual starch reserves but remains, it seems to me, the same plant. Tarbox was now Turbot, but if one peered closely one could perceive the Tarbox within. Same with Arlene. Thor was there. Yet the partial transformations stirred me to reflect cheerfully on our human will to fashion a different and better life.

Two hundred guests feasted on poached turbot and champagne as the atmosphere became more and more buoyant. Sheila, Esther, and I, if not Deronda, were pretty much sloshed when Arlene chimed her goblet and requested silence. *Oh crap, here comes another speech.*

"Baron and I wish to thank all of you for coming. First we'd like to announce our engagement and invite you to the wedding, to take place on Halloween one year from now in the country church at the Farmers' Museum. I'll be given away by the Cardiff Giant."

Laughter.

"You are our two hundred most intimate friends. So I hope nobody will take offense if we single out Sheila Drake, Esther Federman, Jack Thrasher, and Danny Deronda for special thanks. Without the series of blunders, mishaps, and near-death experiences they made possible, I'd still be a man, and Baron and I might never have agreed to tie the knot."

Laughter.

"And now we'd like to announce a new nonprofit initiative, the Institute for the Propagation of Considerable Skepticism Regarding All Evidentiary Claims for Paranormal Phenomena, the IPCSRECPP, pronounced *ipcsrecpp*. Baron declines to be a fellow but will serve as bailiff. So far, nobody's signed up. Look, dearies, there are no dues; we pay you thirty dollars to join."

Muted applause.

"And now, everybody, enough serious talk. I'd like to ask Danny to honor us with his fiddle!"

"I should be willing so to do," Deronda said politely, as he tucked the fiddle under his chin and instantly went into a klezmer bluegrass trance, the wailing and laughing sonorities echoing back from the far recesses of Otsego Lake. This time the Bulgar resulted in no square dancing, and though it wasn't a Jewish wedding, the guests all followed Baron Turbot, who led off the circle dance, joining shoulders with Arlene who joined with Esther who joined with me who joined with Sheila. As was traditional, everyone imitated the steps of the leader, while the circle formed and broke and reformed. Baron had taken lessons in ballroom dancing but was still injecting jitterbug variations. "And this here's the pas de basque," he shouted, leaping and crossing his feet as the guests tried stumblingly to follow suit. Again, the transformation was only partial—Arlene was still given to lumbering and Baron to waddling. But ours was a forgiving company, and the engaged couple finished to loud applause as Arlene gave an awkward bow and Baron waved his stumpy arms in triumph.

* * *

Heading back to the city at breakneck speed thanks to Esther's insouciant approach to space-time, we four reflected nervously on what we'd just witnessed. Sure enough, the women were put out. Each had early on rejected Ohnstad and even precipitated his crisis. But that any man aspiring to their person should have found a plausible fallback in Tarbox was a punch in the ribcage and a stick in the eye. At least this was, I believe, their response on a visceral level, not fully voiced.

"Well, Baron Turbot has some winning qualities," said Sheila weakly.

"Which?" asked Esther, hoping for some validation in Ohnstad's short-lived pursuit of her. She turned her head to the backseat and sped up still more, pushing the Duesenberg to new limits. I clenched.

"Well, he's much improved. He isn't so set in his ways as lots of liberals and yuppies. Tarbox, uh, Turbot doesn't have guile. For white trash, he's rather good."

"Do you suggest he's too simple-minded to have guile?" asked Deronda. "That raises some ethical issues."

"Forget Turbot. What about Arlene?" I asked, knowing full well we couldn't just scrape aside Tarbox, and I was worried that we ourselves might soon need to be scraped off the highway as roadkill. We were approaching a four-leaf clover near Bear Mountain. "Do you think he's reformed or really changed in any way? That new institute, for example, the, uh, IPCSRECPP"—somehow I didn't feel the acronym

would catch on—"he's still bent on exposing people who believe in horoscopes, dowsing, Plant Spirits, Druids, crop circles, UFOs, and the like. Some practical jokester—first he convinces people of the paranormal, then he exposes them for their gullibility."

"Again, this raises some ethical issues," said dour Deronda.

"Yes, but he renounced that tactic—he was really sorry about turning me into a heron. And he donated his Cardiff Giant costume to the Smithsonian."

"Tax write-off, not contrition," opined Deronda.

To be sure, Ohnstad's costume was ironically given a higher appraisal by Sotheby's than the Cardiff Giant himself. They appraised him at one penny per pound—$29.95 plus shipping and handling. The Farmers' Museum then decided against selling the fake.

"Don't you think it takes some courage to go through a sex change?" I asked. "I wouldn't have known Ohnstad had that in him."

Esther turned her head to the backseat again, goosing the accelerator and dipping into what she still coveted by way of Freudian explanation. "Jack, don't conflate psychic needs with moral vir—"

The Duesenberg had just reached the top of the four-leaf clover when she lost control. We sailed off the petal loop into space, the weight of the automobile brushing aside the retaining wall as if it were the balsa wood of Sheila's stage sets. Despite our takeoff speed, it seemed like slow motion as we sailed out in terror, wondering what death would feel like. Sheila must have had a sense of déja tombé. But in her earlier free fall, she was rescued by Tarbox. What we needed now was a choir of angels with fast reflexes.

"Jesus, Es!" I cried.

"Just hold on, guys!"

The Duesenberg continued to arc through the air, rising gracefully then slowly gliding down, as we braced and muttered prayers. I saw the hackneyed radiant golden light at the end of a dark tunnel.

The limousine softly alighted without a sound. We were relieved that death had been painless. Now what?

Lots of white stuff, the clouds of heaven, was swirling about. But I noticed my companions hadn't sprouted wings, and no cherubim and seraphim. Then I ascertained we were moving along the highway, elevated by something or other, making our way down the four-leaf clover in the opposite direction.

"Have we landed on a giant turtle?" asked Sheila.

The entity we landed on came to a halt. It was no turtle. We peered down through the swirl and saw two angry men approach the back of their flat truck. We opened windows.

"Sorry about that," said Esther, choking on the white swirling stuff. "I hope we've not discommoded you. I have some leftover Klonopins."

"Lady, do you know where you've landed? Smack dab on our cargo. There's gonna to be hell to pay."

"What's your cargo?" she asked.

"Organic goose-down featherbeds, bitch. Two hundred and eighty-four of them. Fuckin' expensive."

"Two hundred and eighty-four—that number's pronounced *rapad* in Hebrew—the root means 'to prepare the mattress of love.' And we went off a four-leaf clover! That's for good luck."

"And they're organic!" exclaimed Sheila.

"You two are backsliding," I cautioned. "There's a rational explanation for our soft landing. Yes it's a piece of good luck but, sorry, no suspension of the natural order. With better luck we wouldn't have gone off the road in the first place." Though I had to admit, it was a major miracle to be alive.

"What are you meatheads talking about?" asked one of the truckers. "You've got some explaining to do—to the *fuzz*!"

Meatheads? Fuzz? These truckers were heirs to an antediluvian vocabulary.

"Now see here," said Deronda, "we are quite sorry about what happened. The fault is entirely our own. And it falls to me to take care of any damage to your cargo. I shall simply make out a check. No need to call the . . . fuzz."

"While we're at it, why don't we *buy* some of these organic featherbeds?" suggested Sheila diplomatically.

Tempers abated, and the truckers agreed that this wasn't the time and place to unload a Duesenberg from a flat truck. We settled back in our seats while they drove us on to their destination. This turned out to be the Mohonk Mountain House, an imposing 1890s American Gothic structure that had been recently purchased from the Quaker owners and converted into a federal prison for Enron executives, television evangelicals, celebrity athletes, fracking enthusiasts, and talk show hosts. In purchasing feather beds, the feds were trying to create an environment that would earn the esteem of their inmates. A chain gang of Republicans, which included the recalled state governor, was invited to unload the Duesenberg and damaged featherbeds, to which we owed our very lives. Deronda made out a large check to the truckers and we took our leave.

Maybe it was a normal hesitation about getting back into the Duesenberg with Esther at the wheel, but I suggested we walk down to the quaint gazebo overlooking Lake Mohonk and unwind a bit before driving further. We now had more to ponder, given our near-death experience.

A full moon lit up the lake and surrounding woods to such an extent that we could see the riot of October foliage even at midnight. It was an unusually warm evening. I saw a rowboat cross the diagonal of moonlight on the lake—and in it were two lovers who had snuck the boat out against the rules. Reclining on bamboo chairs, we conversed. I was feeling autumnal.

"Seems like a long time since I first arrived in Cooperstown to check out that giant. So much has happened. I wonder what the moral is," I said, setting the topic and knowing Deronda would have a ready answer.

"The moral is *listen to your mother.*"

Not bad, I thought. Mothers had played quite a role in the lives of Sheila and Esther too. But my own mother, that harridan, I've barely mentioned in this history. And let's face it, there are many not-good-enough mothers in the world.

"What do you think, Es, apart from—how shall I say it?—keeping your eyes on the road."

"Jack, you know I've traded in Kabbalah for mainstream cultural Judaism—and Danny's sense of duty has rubbed off on me." Deronda nodded. "I spend most of my time helping poor old Jews in the Bronx get enough brisket and then helping them get into caskets. No thanks to Freud, I don't fret about my father anymore. And have you noticed? Sheila and I don't fight about who had the harder time of it growing up. We've both got husbands and kids now—that's progress."

I knew from Sheila that Esther had some reservations about Deronda's pajamas and other matters pertaining to the bedroom. It seems that whenever Esther prepared the mattress of love, Deronda broke out his fiddle.

"But what's it all mean?" she continued. "Let me think. Well . . . giving up numerology was hard. It meant the universe was no longer jerry-rigged just for me. I've found different ways of throwing myself into the thick of things."

"Throwing, yes. Sis, let's face it, you've always been reckless."

"But look," said Esther, laughing, "the Doors had it right. We've all broken through to the other side—Ohnstad, Tarbox, you, me, Danny, Jack. We've broken through and are just now finding out what's here. It took hard knocks and flexibility and pluck . . ."

"And luck," I added. "We've all had soft landings instead of our bums getting smushed. No thanks to guardian angels or alignment of the planets. But luck seems like special destiny after one has bounced up like rubber putty. You know, I've decided this is the greatest delusion of all. Every numbskull who becomes president imagines it was his special destiny. This is megalomania. The horoscope is megalomania. Look at Hazel Bouche. Our soft landings and happy endings weren't sure bets—we've been lucky. I think the philosophers call this *contingency*. We could just have easily been characters in a tragic drama."

Sheila weighed in. "But Esther's right. We've added something. We weren't just being bounced about like billiards. My big goof was letting everybody else have the power. It was in my psychic or my Plant Spirit guru, or it was in all the things that were out to get me, toxins, my father—those things had the power—not me."

"Pardon some more backsliding on my part, but it sounds like paranoia," said Esther. "No power. Others out to get you. Remember, sis, you had power over your sets, your costumes, your career. That's what you wanted to be early on—before all the New Age stuff. That Plant Spirit Healer certificate you were working on when you jumped off the balcony—it's an old saying but that certificate plus a subway token could take you to the Bronx. I liked it when we put on costumes at school theatricals—we decided which masks to wear, we played pretend, but it was still us, our faces, beneath the masks. We would come back to ourselves. That's what we've done—come back to ourselves, maybe for the first time because we didn't know how much we already had."

This conversation was getting too solemn and I wasn't sure anybody was making much sense. We all got drowsy as the moon descended, and before we knew it we were asleep.

I was the first to awaken, around six in the morning, and took survey of my slumbering pals. Deronda was humming in his sleep, Sheila was snoring, and Esther was speaking nonsense syllables. I looked out on the tranquil deep-watered lake, cast over by long shadows from trees that ringed it. Ripples appeared near the center. *Trout or pike*, I thought, *having their bug breakfast*. The ripples increased, then a large bulge appeared near the lake's center. The water slowly parted as a *thing* slowly arose. I could make out a dark proboscis, then eyes emerged, then a full head the size of a rhino but shaped like a serpent. The creature turned in my direction and its eyes focused on me. I was paralyzed as in a dream where I wished to cry out and run but couldn't overcome the immense drag of gravity. The long serpentine neck and coiling body set off in our direction, the undulations creating large waves. At about fifty yards it seemed to hesitate, then reared out of the water to a height of about sixty feet. It stood for a moment like a colossus, staring down at me quizzically.

Its forked tongue, at least five feet long, darted out as if in search of giant frogs or maybe people—a serpent licking its chops.

But then it grinned and winked, deciding against eating us, I guess, settling for having given me a good scare. It set off in slow and ponderous undulations to the east.

"Sheila! Esther! Deronda! Wake up! Look there!"

Before I could rouse them, the creature had ducked back under, its long tail waving with a flourish. The ripples that gently cascaded forward and vanished on the rocky beach were the only evidence of a giant beast.

As recent converts to more skeptical ways of thinking, Sheila and Esther said I must be crazy. "Go back to sleep, Jack, you jerk," said Esther. "Please, we're sleepy," said Sheila. Right, tables turned. I readily agreed I was sleepy and crazy and maybe it was a bad dream. I tried to go back to sleep, despite the distant clanging of a Green Party chain gang whipping up their goat cheese omelets and chicory lattes.

There's no evidence I didn't see the Lake Mohonk Monster. Can anybody say I didn't? But I've decided to keep the matter to myself and not dwell on this monster, whom I've named Sally, as I bring this history to a close.

A sneak peek at Larry Lockridge's upcoming novel

The Great Cyprus Think Tank

The island of Cyprus is a world in miniature of what ails the human race. Bart Beasley, a midlist writer of cultural memoirs, forms a think tank of renowned but personally flawed experts. They will address problems still besetting Cyprus in 2024. A fast-paced string of heady and hilarious adventures follows, while romantic liaisons spring up within the ranks. Unknown to all except alert readers is a counterplot to undermine the think tank's best designs.

Prologue

Whenever my dreamworld turns bleak, I glare at my writing desk and cry out to solitary walls, "I'll go abroad!" In early 2022 I was no longer dreaming of sphinxes, pyramids, and caravansaries. My night fantasies had given way to dark frustrations. I couldn't find my classroom and, when I did, was without a syllabus or anything to say, while nameless students peered into iPhones and sullenly drifted off. When I took the elegant stairwell to my gala book launch at the Century Club, I beheld old friends no longer recognizable, for this was our fortieth high school reunion, and I was the emcee. A porter on the Trans Canada told me the Rockies had been leveled because— didn't I know?—Saskatchewan was the new look for Canada. My worst dream was to survey my image in the bathroom mirror and see that I was sixty-two—worst because upon awakening I sighed at its unnerving truth.

The mind beneath mind that is the wellspring of dreams needed fresh water, and I knew where to find it—in the fabled and parched isle of Cyprus.

My doctorate in sociolinguistics has taught me a nonacademic kind of writer's life. I pack my bags and set up in an exotic locale, quickly learn the language and native customs, and within a year or two, produce a novelistic memoir. You may already have read some of them. Thanks for downloading another—Bart Beasley's *The Great Cyprus Think Tank*.

I was born in 1960 in Ottawa but spent four years in Cyprus while my father, a minor Canadian diplomat stationed in Nicosia in 1970, did what he could to make amends for the earlier British occupation of that unfortunate island. He advised the UN Peace Keeping Force in its deployment of Canadian military fodder. Upon the Turkish invasion of 1974 he took credit for deceiving the Turks and protecting the airport in Nicosia by telling the Canadians to move their pitiable handful of tanks around all night as noisily as possible, with bright lights. Good thinking. The Turks concluded the airport was too heavily fortified to bother with, at least at the time. But the invasion was so stressful that my father suffered a mild coronary and was sent home to Ottawa along with his wife and me, their only child. He died not long after.

Having clocked the years from ten to fourteen there, I found that Cyprus had lodged deep in my memory cells and re-emerged from time to time as a yearning. In 2022 it beckoned again.

As you know, to the amazement of everybody the world over, the island was reunified earlier that year. In a new pan-Cypriot bi-communal federation, restrictions on travel across the border imposed by the Turks in 1974 were lifted. Resettlement of displaced Greek Cypriots and Turkish Cypriots was soon underway, with somewhat less gory jousting over old homesteads than might have been expected. But ethnic animosities persisted, as did other worries—desertification, a diet dominated by British chips, a rising sea level that threatened hatcheries of the famed sea turtles, the slaughter of migratory songbirds, and looting of antiquities for sale on the black market.

I'm not by nature a social engineer or utopianist. One motive was frankly self-interest in whipping up fresh material for this memoir. But I'd also felt at times an urge to do my species some good beyond fictionalized memoirs that leave little trace beyond an evening's frolic in the minds of a handful of pale, unsatisfied readers seeking ports of call they can never visit because too poor, infirm, or lazy. Then too, there were deficits in my life that prompted my conscience to acts of compensation.

I applied to the Soros foundation to fund a think tank. Let me enlist specialists to rescue the island, I told them. It took only a few hours on the internet to seek out the world's finest, some of them already familiar with the island, and add their names to the application form. They included a zoologist, a nutritionist, a meteorologist, a neurologist, and an archeologist. My project may smack of presumptuous American world-beating, but keep in mind that I'm Canadian.

The Soros foundation knew a good idea when it saw one and, within weeks, was depositing large sums in my checking account at Chase on lower Broadway. This wasn't my money, but it felt good to see my account plump up beyond a midlist author's best imagining. I was teaching creative nonfiction at NYU as an adjunct and barely paying rent for a modest one-bedroom at 68 Carmine Street.

I'll spare you two years of logistics. The Cyprus Think Tank took up residence in Káthikas, a small village in the west overlooking ancient Páphos. We numbered five geniuses plus me.

You may already know us from the singular episodes we occasioned during our brief tenure on the island, having gained influence within the new pan-Cypriot government. The Minister of the Interior was amused by my scheme, viewing it as crackbrained but harmless enough. And she was happy to receive a handsome subsidy from Soros, which could have purchased the entire island with cash on hand.

My special interest in Cyprus, beyond saving it and writing this memoir, was the literary connections—not native writers but the outsiders Arthur Rimbaud and Lawrence Durrell, who lived for brief spells on the island. The French poet was the negative lure, Durrell the positive. Rimbaud gave up verse at the age of twenty as the most precocious writer in the history of literature. He turned his back on the whole enterprise. What boots it? Whenever I suffer writer's block, I say to myself, *Rimbaud knew he need not write more, so why should I?* Durrell kept writing beyond *The Alexandria Quartet*, but never again so well.

I had good reason to believe that Rimbaud left a notebook on Cyprus. I wanted that notebook, I wanted it! And I wanted to visit Béllapais in the North where Durrell had lived, thinking his shade might breathe words into me. I needed them.

Another lure was William Shakespeare, most of whose *Othello* is set in Cyprus, probably Famagusta. I couldn't know early on how much this tragic drama would impinge on my farce.

In its contradictions Cyprus is a haunting enigma. Yes, it has everything—from splendid antiquities of the many cultures that have flourished there, to an enchanted geography of mountains, deserts, and beaches, to legendary cities, monasteries, mosques, and castles, to the celebrated haloumi cheese and zivanía brandy. But it suffers the worst consequences of climate change, the ethnic enmities that have spilt kraters of blood and still simmer here and there, the loathsome residue of rapacious mining and industry, the public-health menace of a greasy British diet, and the geopolitical disadvantage of proximity to both the Middle East and Africa, a pawn caught in the interplay of larger powers. It's not much of a stretch to say that in Cyprus we find Planet Earth in miniature. After the ordeals of Brexit, with its improbable focus on a 310-mile internal Irish border, and the coronavirus pandemic, with its promiscuous feasting on a 24,901-mile ring of hapless humans, I feel it's time to return Cyprus to the map of global awareness. If you stick with my memoir, you'll be getting a parable of the human race in the early twenty-first century for ninety-nine cents.

And I promise you adventures I couldn't have made up, including dark forces intent on sabotaging my benevolent scheme. I admit to having little imagination but do have a memoirist's habit of jotting everything down at day's end. If you doubt my reliability, I've taken inspiration from Rimbaud and have tucked my own notebook somewhere in the vast library of the Oneida Community Mansion House in upstate New York, where my story ends and where I wrote this memoir over a period of three weeks. If you find my notebook, read it and decide for yourself whether I have exaggerated. But the staff doesn't permit removal of anything from their library, even for private reading in one of their rental rooms. A ghostly impersonator of the Oneida Community founder, John Humphrey Noyes, will track down and bring to justice anybody who violates this rule. Unless you relish confronting a religious lunatic, I'd advise you to let my notebook rest unmolested among the relics of print culture that gather dust in the stately Mansion House left by the polyamorous utopians, who remind us that utopias come but mostly go.

Ingram Content Group UK Ltd.
Milton Keynes UK
UKHW040720280323
419285UK00005B/446